SEEDS OF WISDOM

BY

STEFAN MONTROSE

DEDICATION

To you the reader, and to those
that have motivated and inspired me.
Thank you.

ACKNOWLEDGEMENT

I thank all those who throughout my life have contributed to my training and make me what I have become today: God, my family, my teachers, my colleagues, my friends, and everyone I have met on my way. I am also indebted to a large number of books, and I cannot thank their authors enough for their sharing and generosity.

TABLE OF CONTENTS

1.

BROKEN CIGARETTE.

From within him, he felt his heart sank to the deepest pit of his bowels. Fear consumed every last fragment of bravery in his frail body. He knew that this time, he couldn't squirm his way out of this one. His throat grew arid, and his chest taut as his mind began brainstorming different forms of punishment, each more horrible than the first.

Suddenly an uncanny noise penetrated his concentration, a sound that caused his heart to beat thunderously. It was the sound of heels clapping against the floor. Ruthlessly they met the ceramic floor, abusing it with all manner of disrespectful curses. The sound echoed down the hall, the wearers paces growing swifter and more aggressive. As the sound grew closer, beads of sweat began to trail down his face.

The door behind him swiftly opened, and he refused the unrelenting urge to turn and view who had just entered. The heels continued its diatribe on the tile floor walking around him. Grudgingly his eyes quickly caught the sight of a rather tall, skinny, brown-skinned woman. She was clothed in a cloud white cotton dress. The boy noticed that it matched the white streaks of hair that she styled neatly into a bun. Her deep black hair made the white more prominent. She quickly sat and uneasily made herself cozy, with the chair squeaking in agony until she finally sank into the black leather chair.

Her black eyes stared at him pensively, her slim face twisted into a grimace of disgust. The silence was long and tense, in that time the boy's back and armpits grew damp with sweat, nervously he would mop his brows with the back of his hands, while he kept his eyes glued to the table that separated him from the school dean.

"This is becoming most tedious, don't you think, Mr. Jabari?" she said in a stern voice, shattering the silence. Jabari rose his eyes, quickly glanced at her, then returned them to the table and said nothing. She paused, earnestly looking at him as though anticipating an answer.

"It seems you enjoy our encounters because you continue to flout!" She rose her voice, increasing the tension. Jabari fought hard to avoid eye contact, for he knew if he looked at her face, he would shatter. "Well I," his voice croaked, and his throat seized.

"Are you speaking to the table!" she snarled at him.

Immediately, he looked up and saw a menacing glare, and shallow reddened cheeks, owing to anger. Jabari's belligerent tongue, tied into a rather large knot, and his mind sped into overdrive thinking of all the various methods of punishment that was about to ensue. He could hear Mrs. White's heels incessantly tapping on the tile floor, with each tap more aggressive than the last. For each time her heel hit the floor, an ounce of patience left her body.

"Well isn't this a sight, Jabari is lost for words, unbelievable," she said with a sly grin brimmed across her face.

"But hopefully this would make you talk," she said, looking down to her desk and pulling open her drawer. The wooden drawer dragged loudly and with great resistance. It let out a sound similar to that of dragging fingers on a chalkboard. Jabari cringed and began muttering all manner of prayers his mind could imagine. Mrs. White fished violently through its contents until she paused. A pleased look formed on her long face, and she grabbed something out quickly and kept it concealed in her bony hands. She then moved her hands over the table and said, "look, boy!" Sluggishly she released her bony fingers, and a small damaged cigarette fell on the table.

"Speak!" She muttered, as her evidence hit the table. Jabari was flabbergasted, his mind throbbed with questions. "How did she? Who spoke? When did she?"

Tears began to well up in his eyes, but he managed to keep them at bay, he rubbed his nose violently to curb himself from crying.

He took a deep breath, "I, my grandfather has a habit, he asked me to buy some for him, they say it's bad, and I gave him one less and kept the other in my pocket and forgot it," Jabari stuttered.

He paused, the tears were tugging on his eyelids, so he again rubbed his nose, snorted and pulled the mucus that was running down his nostrils.

"I only remembered I had it in my pocket later on and pulled it out in front of everyone. They thought it was mine, and I didn't deny; I played along. But when I heard there was going to be a mass search in school, I threw it under my desk, and when I came back, it was gone." Jabari stopped, for the first time in a while, he was veracious, he felt a sense of ease, that he had long forgotten.

Mrs. White looked at him, watching intensely for any subtle movements which might indicate fallacy in his narrative. There

3

was another painfully silent pause in which Jabari and Mrs. White glared at each other. Then she sighed, and said to him, "You are free to go, however, if I find out you are lying, or I find another one of these and I could pin it to you, expulsion! Do I make myself clear!" Mrs. White said hardheartedly.

Jabari nodded, and with haste got out of the office, his mind in ecstasy, happy that he got out without consequence. With swiftness in his steps, he trailed to the bin outside the school's compound, clawing his pockets, throwing away the cigarettes that were buried there.

2.

ZAHEER'S PLIGHT.

Instincts took control, and before he knew, his fist met his enemy's face with a large thud. His foe's head flew back with the collision of knuckles smashing into his cheek. For a moment, Zaheer felt a rush of power and bliss. He clenched his teeth hard and smiled, ignoring the searing pain from his bleeding knuckles. The spectators around him roared, but before he could bathe his ego in their praise, his opponent rose, for he had much to lose if he gave up so easily.

His opponent reached for a broken chair, and a leg fell out in his hand. Though he had no intention of using it, he was desperate; he couldn't lose this fight, not to this 'imps', he would lose his position of power. So, he rose up and swung hard. The chair leg slammed across Zaheer's face with such an impact that he jerked back, and the thud echoed as the crowd grew silent in disbelief at what they've just witnessed.

Zaheer's body flew off-balance, His knees buckled, and a sense of numbness overtook him before the pain set in. His head pulsed in heat and searing soreness. He could feel the streams of blood trailing down his face and staining his white school shirt.

Zaheer despised the thought of going to school. Slowly he wormed himself into the uniform; the overly large white shirt and

5

long grey trousers. The hem of his trousers was worn from constantly being dragged beneath his shoe. With no zeal nor vigor, Zaheer forced his feet into his crisp snow-white sneakers. He glanced at the mirror, his eyes scanning himself briefly, then in frustration he sucked his teeth.

From the first week, he learned that school was no longer a place of innocence and joyousness like his days in primary school, but more so a place of tumult, ridicule and segregation. His emotions grew calluses, from being taunted about his looks, the branding of his shoe and the floppiness of his uniform.

As he entered the gate, the heckling would start, "Watch how black he is nah he has a hue," one said, followed by a chorus of laughter. "What kind of shoe is that, look at his uniform," said another wickedly. Zaheer, however, remained silent, marinating in anger and shame. He would clench his jaw tight and failed each time to convince himself it didn't affect him.

Following his usual routine, he slowly and silently walked to class. Strolling to the back, away from the various clusters of students to be by himself. He planted himself firmly in the wooden desk and glared out the window enjoying what minute sense of peace he had.

"A, A, look the black shit!" Tobi exclaimed as he entered the class followed by his clique, who roared in scandalous laughter.

Zaheer sucked his teeth hard and remained unfazed looking out the window.

"Black shit! black shit!"

"You eh hear I'm calling you!!" Tobi shouted louder and louder, in an attempt to antagonize Zaheer.

Zaheer continued looking out the window, not paying him any attention.

He squeezed his fist tightly and tried his best to ignore the heckling.

Tobi, unsatisfied, and enjoying the attention he was receiving, went into his girlfriend's bag, her name was Jenna, who, uncomfortable with the entire scene, looked away. Tobi reached for a roll of toilet paper and rushed to Zaheer. His face grew red and wore a crazed smile of rage and mischief. He then tore a sheet of the paper and rubbed Zaheer's shoulder and said, "Shit, you hear me calling you!"

With that, the crowd screamed with laughter, the girls too. Jenna chuckled uncomfortably, for her eyes couldn't conceal her look of concern for Zaheer.

The boy continued to ignore, moving his hands while getting up to move away from Tobi.

"Where you going!" Tobi flared up his chest as though to intimidate him.

Tobi was much bigger than Zaheer in comparison, and his reputation for trouble and fighting preceded him, and any chance he saw to prove his strength, he rose to the occasion. As Zaheer attempted to leave, Tobi blocked his path and pushed him back.

Zaheer stumbled a bit, but his footing remained rooted.

"Yesterday you played you were answering me back and cursing me under your breath, you have no respect, talking to Jenna, with your bootleg shoes, and shit face," said Tobi.

Zaheer looked Tobi in the eye and glared in anger; his patience was running thin. Over the last four months, he was insulted and pushed around by Tobi and stayed silent, but ignoring him was becoming more arduous with each passing day.

"Aye, who are you looking at?" Tobi said, flexing his chest to look bigger. He took the roll of toilet paper and struck Zaheer in his head.

The crowd roared and he could hear a voice in the crowd say, "Now it's just to flush."

Instincts took control, and before he knew, his fist met his enemy's face with a large thud. His foe's head flew back with the collision of knuckles smashing into his cheek. For a moment, Zaheer felt a rush of power and bliss. He clenched his teeth hard and smiled, ignoring the searing pain from his bleeding knuckles. Briefly, he noticed the audience around him, roaring in excitement. Tobi was in shock as he could feel the blood fill his mouth.

Zaheer felt a sense of elation he never knew. His nerves winced in excitement. A broad smile stretched across his face as he began to bask in silencing the hecklers. At this time, word had reached all corners of the school beckoning a crowd eager to see two fools pummel each other. The masses began to cheer Zaheer.

But before he could bathe his ego in their praise, his opponent rose, for he had much to lose if he gave up so easily.

His opponent reached for a broken chair, and a leg fell out in his hand. Though he had no intention of using it, he was desperate; he couldn't lose this fight, not to this 'imps' he would lose his position of power. So, he rose and swung hard. The chair leg slammed across Zaheer's face with such an impact that he jerked back, and the thud echoed as the crowd grew silent in disbelief at what they've just seen.

Zaheer's body flew off-balance, his knees buckled, and a sense of numbness overtook him before the pain set in. His head pulsed in heat and searing soreness. He could feel the streams of blood trailing down his face and staining his white school shirt.

Tobi, for a moment, wore a face of concern as blood engulfed his opponent's face, but quickly, he forced a grimace of anguish and pleasure. Zaheer hunched over, clenching his head in shock at the pain. Tobi, to capitalize on the crowd's astonishment, continued with the broken leg in his hand, aiming to assault his broken foe.

But in response to the pain, adrenaline pumped in Zaheer's body, heightening his reflexes. To Tobi's dismay, Zaheer caught the leg in mid-strike. He hauled it from the hands of his foe, and with great force threw it into the crowd. He could hear the screams as many in the audience took cover and cursed at the projectile. The leg landed solidly on the head of one of Tobi's steadfast supporters knocking him cold onto the ground. Tobi grew steadily apprehensive at what was in front of him. The left of Zaheer's face was drenched in blood and the right with sweat. Zaheer clenched his teeth and growled as he rushed towards Tobi. Panic handicapped Tobi's movements so much so, that his foe connected one blow to his face, then another to his throat.

Tobi fell flat on his back, clenching his neck with both hands. Fighting to breathe, he coughed profusely, choking on his saliva. Zaheer took the opportunity to huddle over Tobi, allowing his anger to overtake him, he clenched his fist and continuously pummelled his foe's face. Before long Tobi's face was marred with bruises and blood. So engulfed with rage, he had not noticed the scampering of the crowd nor the summoning of the school's security. He could only feel the hands grab around his chest, snatching him off the badly beaten Tobi. Zaheer didn't even notice Tobi had passed out. But in the crowd, he could hear screams as they assumed Zaheer had killed Tobi. The children shuddered as they dragged Tobi's limped body, trying to revive him in the process.

"Take them to the nurse quickly!"

"And the Dean, call her!" the security said roughly, gasping for air as he struggled to restrain an incensed Zaheer.

Two guards lifted Tobi and quickly headed in the direction of the nurse's office. Zaheer's, anger had slowly begun to quell as he realized that the dean was going to be informed. His sight had narrowed, and as he looked around, all he could see were eyes of fright and amazement. In a strange way he welcomed this reverence from them, they respected his strength.

As they both entered the nurse's office, she immediately phoned an ambulance for them both. The Dean who was already there waiting, merely glanced at the two of them and said sternly, "I will accompany them both to the hospital!"

Gingerly the nurse tended to the blood on Zaheer's face and ensured that Tobi was stable and breathing, though unconscious; owing more to fright than to the blows.

The Dean all the while remained silent, just scanning, her eyes pensively darting from Zaheer to Tobi.

Zaheer fought hard for their eyes not to meet, he glanced at every nook and crevice of the room hoping to rest his eyes on a comforting sight.

"He will need stitches! What the hell he hit you with?" the nurse said in deep concern.

Zaheer was hesitant, but he answered under his breath, "A chair leg."

"Speak up boy!" the dean roared.

"A chair leg Miss Stewart."

A chorus of gasp and chants beckoning God himself followed by all except the dean, who remained silent.

"And the other, what of him?" the Dean asked dryly.

"Unconscious and bruised badly but…," during the dean's inquiry she heard the blaring of the siren.

"The ambulance is here!" one of the assistants in the nurse's office exclaimed.

"Make sure they don't leave without me, give me a moment to prepare," the dean said to the assistant with her eyes glaring at Zaheer.

Quickly the attendant from the ambulance came in, the attendant gingerly strapped Tobi to the bed and then ushered Zaheer to the ambulance as well.

"I took the liberty of getting your stuff and phoning both your parents, so they will meet us at the hospital. Once there, you will explain to me what happened. Based on that, I would decide what to do further," the dean said, as she climbed into the ambulance and sat on the opposite side of Zaheer.

Zaheer grew uneasy as he knew his mother and father would not appreciate this circumstance. He immediately began to rehearse his alibi, ensuring to leave out parts that would impeach him. He looked over to Tobi, whose nose and mouth was housed behind an oxygen mask, though he felt a strong sense of satisfaction, he knew his parents and Tobi's, won't take lightly of this.

Two hours slowly elapsed as Zaheer sat on the hospital bed in deep contemplation on the events of the fight in his head. He was

11

being treated behind curtains, next to him was the still, silent Tobi. When he had received the final stitch, his mother burst in, her eyes teary. "Is this what I'm sending you to school for!!" she said, her voice thundering throughout the ward. Her large voice made up for her little stature.

"Ms. Mills, please calm down," the dean said in a cool calm voice as she trailed in behind her. The dean's tall lean figure towered behind Ms. Mills'.

"Where is the other child?" she asked concerned.

Before the dean could respond, Ms. Mills darted to the bed next door.

"My God!" she exclaimed, covering her mouth in revulsion. In anguish she made a beeline to her son, and snatched him by his shirt collar.

"Don't kill him yet," the dean said.

"What happened here?" Ms. Mills asked.

"You will find out once Tobi's guardian arrives," replied the dean.

"Yes, I eagerly await the discussion of the incident," Zaheer's mother said as she released his collar and calmed herself. Zaheer felt shame and anger. His anger, however, was aimed towards his mother. He pondered on the numerous lamentations he made to her about Tobi prior to this occurrence, and she constantly ignored him, and when he finally defended himself, she is angry at him. His resentment festered and resulted in him kissing his teeth. As the sound reached her ear, his mother turned around ready to slap him, but the arrival of Tobi's mother and father spared him.

Tobi's mother was rather attractive. She was short and shapely, her voice was harsh and coarse, and it seemed she rushed to the hospital, as her bundles weren't properly styled. His father wore an aggressive expression. He wore baggy expensive clothing and chains of gold perched loosely around his neck. Tobi's father's gaze remained fixed on Zaheer. Their eyes met, and Zaheer began to fidget as he could feel his intent to damage him.

"Thank you for coming. Now, before we proceed further, your sons were in a fight. As you know, Tobi is a repeat offender, and allegedly he incites fights." The dean calmly addressed the parents, but her speech was then interrupted by Tobi's mother:

"Listen, my son doesn't start anything. Look at the state of my child. Does he look like somebody who started something? He's unconscious and bedridden, and the next one only has one cut."

The dean rose her brows in annoyance, "Can I please proceed?" She paused, looked to both parties, and continued, "Thank you, he is a repeated offender and this is not the first time he and Zaheer had a disagreement. However, this is the first time the results are what we see before us today."

"And what are you going to do about this? Because if you aren't doing anything about it, I could," Tobi's father said, looking at Zaheer.

Ms. Mills flared her nose and looked at Mr. Hall. "Hello, you would leave the disciplining of my child to me. If what the dean says is true, then, you are not very good at it with your son."

The dean interjected saying, "Hello, both of you, if this is the way you as parents react, it's no wonder your children are like this!" the dean glowered back at the parents.

13

"Now please allow me to finish, thank you!" she said sternly, and both parents grew silent and listened.

"Based on what I've said about Tobi's background, it would be easy to dismiss this entire thing as a provocation, however, I would not have Zaheer return to school and be a hero of sorts for violence; he should have walked away."

"Tried to!" Zaheer shouted.

"Quiet!" The dean roared at him.

Ms. Mills gave him a fierce look, its intent to silence Zaheer.

Zaheer clenched his fist, bit his tongue, and looked away at the floor.

"Nor would I have Tobi return to school scot-free as though he is invincible, though it would be fitting justice for him to return to school humbled."

"What nonsense am I hearing?" Tobi's father outburst.

"Look, listen, Janice, I can't listen to this 'shit'. When you are done talking to this 'waste of time' teacher, come meet me in the car cause if I stay here, I will get ignorant." Tobi's father said, barking to his wife, then he turned on his heel and bounced off in a rebellious fashion.

The dean formed a face of such disdain at the sight of the man's reaction. Zaheer fought the urge to chuckle as he looked at the dean's face, but he simply kept his head down and listened.

"Continue please," Zaheer's mother said.

"Yes Ms. Mills as I was saying before ignorance reared its head, I propose, as a means to avoid this ever occurring again that they are transferred, effective immediately, that is, if no charges would be placed on them both. Given the extent of their actions, they are to be suspended and the police would get involved."

Both parents remained calm and quiet. Zaheer however, gawked at the dean, for her words stunned him.

Transferred, Charged, he pondered.

Ms. Mills looked to her son, "Charge his ass," she said.

Zaheer's eyes widened, but he said nothing, he fiercely bantered, screamed and shouted expletives in his mind at her.

"Ms. Mills, please reconsider this carefully, this would be a blemish on his record that would remain with him for the rest of his life, both their lives," she said, looking to both parents.

Tobi's mother looked over and simply said, "Transfer my son please."

Reluctantly, Ms. Mills looked over to Zaheer, "Move him too, though I have a right to keep him there, put a stain on your school's reputation because I know you want to handle this quietly to protect that."

The dean bore an uncomfortable look on her slim pale face.

"If you are transferring him, I want him closer to home and in a school of higher prestige." Ms. Mills continued.

The dean nodded, "Come with me, and I will explain the details."

The parents and the dean then left the room, and Zaheer was left to stare at Tobi.

"Dumb idiot I hope they beat you up every day where they send you," he said snidely hoping Tobi would hear him. But all he could hear was his laboured breathing.

He got off his bed, rubbing the stitched laceration on his head as the pain subsided a bit.

He began to ponder to himself, walking towards the window of the hospital room.

"I am wrong, you tease me, when I defended myself, I am the wrong one, I don't regret beating your ass," he said rubbing the stitches.

"But in a way, I'm glad for a new start, I won't let anyone take advantage of me this time!" Zaheer said in a rage.

"Zaheer!!" His mother shouted, "Come now!" Slowly he walked out towards his mother's voice glaring in rage at Tobi.

The woman trailed off with such haste that he struggled to keep up. But as he opened the door, his eyes met Jenna. Her eyes were swollen and red, her brown cheeks were puffy, clearly crying didn't agree with her, or it was something her body wasn't acclimatized too. Zaheer froze, forgetting his mom. He stood ashamed moving his hands into his pockets. He tried to form words but he merely mouthed awkwardly. Jenna wiped her eyes and said, "I'm sorry, sorry, I wanted to come in but I," she paused momentarily to wipe her nose.

Zaheer's eyes remained fixed at her, even in sadness, he still noticed her; how pretty she was. She blushed slightly as she rose to look at him to continue her lament. "I hated not doing anything, I felt helpless, I chose to be, I allowed Tobi too, we all did, and because of that you both are hurt and here. I know most likely you won't be here any longer, both of you, but I just wanted to tell you, I wanted you to know." She then paused again, struggling to hold back tears.

"Wherever you go, don't become like Tobi, don't be a bully, don't be like me, and good luck." She reached out to hug him and grasped him so hard his cheeks turned purple.

She quickly let go of him and ran to Tobi's bed. Zaheer stood there frozen, unaware that his mother was close by listening, she walked towards him and gently laid her hand on his shoulder. She looked at him, merely eyeing him with a look of remorsefulness, then they both walked towards the waiting room where the dean awaited them patiently.

3.

FIRE AND SALT

T he nights were colder than usual; the wind pierced his very skin and etched his bones. He tossed and turned relentlessly in his mahogany bed. There was nothing but silence; the usual orchestra of crickets was quiet tonight. "This is the coldest it has ever been since I moved to Trinidad!" Chavez whispered to himself in anger. Frustrated, Chavez crawled from his bed and walked out to the veranda, there was an uneasiness in the air. The trees rustled and shuffled as the cold air tumbled through them.

Chavez glared at the night sky, which was clear of cloud and stars. Only the full moon to meet his gaze. He thought to himself; *why can't I sleep?* His heavy eyes scanned the area, overlooking the canopy of trees; the tall bamboos, the banana clusters, the cocoa trees, and the sugar cane fields. His eyes finally stopped at the barracks and its very sight made him melancholy. He never fancied the idea of owning a plantation and slaves, and up to the present day it still never sat well in his mind.

Chavez had inherited the house and plantation from his father, who passed away in his sleep. The house had first belonged to his great-great-grandfather Hugo Alvarado, who was a retired conquistador. Chavez, however, never truly wanted to come to Trinidad. He had always preferred the comfort of Spain over the untamed Caribbean.

He exhaled firmly and decided to retreat to his bed once more when suddenly, a scream came from the barracks. He turned, quickly straining his eyes, in the hopes that he could deduce the commotion. The scream grew louder, and a stampede of slaves ran out of the barracks. Chavez ran inside and reached under his mahogany bed for his rifle, for he thought it was some manner of revolt. In his alacrity, he stormed out of his room, forgetting to throw on shoes or trousers. His footsteps thundered down the stairs and onto the hard wooden floors. He reached for the lock and swung the door open quickly and clenched the rifle tighter in his hand.

He made a beeline towards his hounds. Eagerly, each barked in excitement as he released them from their cages, and gingerly they trailed behind him towards the barracks. As he approached the enclosure, he slowed his pace. His bare feet sank into the cold, muddy earth and he silently scolded himself for forgetting to wear shoes. The slaves jumped in fear as they heard and saw the battalion of dogs. He stopped in front of the entrance and the dogs halted, sniffing the air, patiently awaiting his command. Chavez slowly entered, his stomach made a knot, he raised the rifle and kept his finger near the cold trigger. The other hand clasped the cold, dusty rifle. Sweat began to trail down his face, he turned his head and whistled to beckon his hounds. They quickly followed on the alert, with their ears erected, and body tensed. The slaves that remained in the barracks remained cemented to the walls, ensuring to procure as much space between them, Chavez and the hounds.

The smell of fire and smoke rushed to his nostrils as he continued in the barracks. Chavez's eyes opened wide at the sight of a slave hunched over; he was dead. Delicately, he moved closer towards the corpse. His dark skin was pale and his face frozen in fear. His eyes slowly searched for any sign of trauma. Until they managed to catch sight of a peculiar wound on his neck. It was severely charred. Chavez's face contorted into a grimace of revulsion. Quickly, he turned on his heel and shouted, "What happened here!"

A slave woman named Maria came out of the corner and spoke to the crowd. Upon completion of her inquiry, Maria walked over to Chavez, "A ball of fire, a big ball of fire; it came inside the barracks and attacked Liam, it went for his neck," she reported, after which a long-drawn frown was engraved upon her face.

Chavez stared at her, confused; "Balls of fire don't attack people!" he said in contempt, his voice bellowing to every corner of the barracks.

"Maria, please find out who killed this man!" he continued, the blood still boiling in his veins. Maria's sad frown turned into a rude smirk, but she did as he had asked. Chavez didn't particularly understand the creole spoken on this island, it was a mixture of Spanish, French, and English, all merged with the African speech. But he could pick up the apparent attitude in Maria's tone as she translated his request.

He turned to the dogs, scanning them as they sifted the air. Chavez himself began to look for any clues. This was to no avail as there were no blood trails and no wounds on his body, just the burnt markings on his neck. He looked at the slaves, their eyes were filled with a mixture of animosity and dread towards him, "The ball of fire killed Liam," Maria said rudely. Chavez exhaled; "Maria, tell them to bury the body, I would have a priest come in

20

the morning." Chavez left the barracks and went back into the house. "Ball of fire," he spoke to himself, glancing back at the slaves and the barracks.

The next day Chavez went into his records. He looked through the listings of all the slaves who currently resides, and previously lived on the plantation. Mountains of dusty tomes were stacked at his feet as he fished through a sea of pages. In his search he uncovered their lineage and their descendants. He discovered that Liam was the father of two children; Lionel and Lisille. Both worked alongside him in the cane fields. At the funeral, there was a deafening silence, not a slave cried, not even his children. He found this unusual, but he placed the thought in the deepest recesses of his mind.

After the funeral, he proceeded to the veranda and surveyed the plantation. His sight set squarely on his labor force. The slave drivers and slaves worked ferociously. He hunched over the railing in the veranda and strained his eyes, hoping to observe them in more detail. But what he saw were semblances of disdain and despondency from their body language. "Master Chavez?" Maria called, as she entered the veranda, "Yes Maria, to what do I owe the pleasure?" he replied.

Maria acted as his eyes and ears on the plantation. The slaves respected and trusted her. She also acted as Chavez's translator and his guide to understanding the plantation and the people. Chavez scanned her brown skin and the long blue dress she wore, which accentuated her voluptuous figure. Her hair was wrapped and kept concealed under a white cloth. "They say it's the work of an evil Soucouyant," she said.

"Foolishness!" Chavez scoffed, "There is no such thing!" "Si, oui, Master Chavez!" Maria replied in the same tone. Irritated by this, he immediately left the veranda and went into his room to cool his thoughts. His mind flashed back to the letters from his father he received whilst in Spain. These letters held accounts of a strange creature that his father would see in his dreams, a beast made of fire, which the locals called, the Soucouyant.

"Silliness!" he muttered aloud. Maria, who was eavesdropping, jumped in fear alerting Chavez. Their eyes met, "Sorry about my manners Maria, forgive me," Chavez said, bowing his head in shame. "Master Chavez, it's fine," she said with a genuine smile across her face. Chavez humbled himself and sat on the wooden chair near his bed. "Tell me about this creature; this Soucouyant," he asked Maria. Maria's face brimmed with a strange excitement and her eyes widened. Maria answered, "The Soucouyant is a woman, sometimes an old woman who deals in evil, she's human in the day, but when the Soleil; the sun goes down, she sheds her skin and she sucks 'yuh' blood or might even kill you." Chavez couldn't help but sneer at this story, "Thank you, Maria, that would be all." "Merci," she replied and trailed off.

Once more, the screams of slaves came in the dead of night, and Chavez drew his rifle once again. Ten slave drivers were found dead, their skins burnt but their bodies were cold. Maria again forewarned that it was the doing of this creature. This, of course, annoyed Chavez. He searched diligently for evidence, but to no avail; there was nothing to support any other explanation.

Defeated from the failed search, he sluggishly moved towards the house, when suddenly he noticed the boy Lionel busily clearing the fields of weeds and dry leaves. "Lionel! Lionel!" Chavez beckoned him, waving his arms to garner his attention. The boy winced and gazed back flabbergasted, then quickly ran towards him, tripping on his feet thrice.

"Yes, yes master," he said timidly.

"Lionel, sorry about your father's death, it's not easy for a boy to lose his father."

The boy said nothing, he merely moved his eyes to his feet.

"Lionel, I know you must be still grieving, but if there is anything, anything at all you know that could help me find out who killed him-"

"No, No, I know nothing," he said fidgeting, quickly he glanced to the edge of the field then, back to Chavez.

Chavez sighed, "Okay, but if you notice anything, anything strange, let me know, okay?" he said, raising his eyebrows, gazing intensely at the boy.

Lionel quickly shook his head, then ran back to his work.

Early Monday morning, he quickly left the plantation and went into Port of Spain. His destination was the Government House to file a complaint. Upon his arrival, he was greeted by a procession of plantation owners from around the vicinity. They were complaining about the same issue. "Chavez, you are having the same problem as well?" This question came from William Quashie; a friend of Chavez. He was a Creole born, with French and Spanish roots, much like Chavez. "So many problems this year," he continued, "1820 is not the year to own a plantation. They stopped the slave trade, and now someone is murdering the slaves," he lamented, his plumb face red in anger after his ranting.

The Government House doors were shut tightly, and the officials placed a notice on the front doors stating; *We are aware of your grievances and have sent your complaints to the Monarchy, help will come, God bless the Queen*. This incensed the owners even more, and their ranting turned into bitter cursing.

23

"That is not good enough, the queen cares not for us!" one angry planter said as he mocked the notice. "I know you are there, you better come out and help us!" said another while banging on the door. Chavez foreboded a riot and thought it best to head home. "It seems I have to seek out this killer myself," he said to himself as he rode his horse back home.

That night Chavez took his pillow, rifle, and his six hounds all with him to sleep in the barracks. The barracks were wooden cottage-like buildings with thatched roofs. Littered inside were mahogany beds, planted firmly on the floor. Three buildings were dedicated to the slave residents. The first was for children and the elderly, the second; where the deaths mostly occurred, was assigned to the men, and the third for the women. Chavez cleverly or more foolishly decided to perch in the second. He placed three hounds each outside, and the other three at the entrance of the garrisons.

The slaves were quite uneased and suspicious of Chavez's presence amongst them. They treated him as though he had some disease, some even chose to sleep on the floor, rather than be in proximity to him. The smell of rotting wood and salted fish tickled his nose in revulsion but his resolve didn't meander. Despite the cold and hard wooden floor, he tossed and managed to find a comfortable spot and laid silent. Before he knew it, his eyes grew heavy and he slowly drifted into a deep slumber.

In his dream, he was in Spain, walking along the concrete brick road. He dawned a broad wide smile on his pale face as he greeted his Spanish kin. Free of the worries of the Caribbean, he walked with extra vigor. Then suddenly in his dream, he began to feel a peculiar heat, sweat beaded his face and his body grew damp. In shock and fear, his eyes caught a vicious flame that engulfed everything around him. The cheerful denizens that littered the

24

bricked road were now screaming in agony, their bodies engulfed in fire. Chavez's eyes widened and he felt his neck sear in pain, quickly, he began to claw his neck in an attempt to ease the pain. But as his fingers met his skin, his hands were covered in a crimson flame.

Chavez quickly woke up, his body soaked in perspiration, he touched his neck and turned around to scan the area. To his dismay, his eyes met a hideous sight. A howling scarlet ball of fire hovered near him.

His jaw dropped, and his body seized. The pain on his neck was unimaginable. He clasped his hand around it and he could feel the blistered and charred flesh. He mustered all the strength he could but managed to only twitch his fingers. In frustration, he roared, "God in heaven I need you!" The creature screamed at the desperate man's words and flew swiftly out of the barrack window, leaving behind shimmers of fire on the floor, and a noxious smog in the air. Chavez's eyes burned as they readjusted to the surroundings, and his body felt heavy as he slowly tried to lift it. He also noticed that he was alone, the slaves were gone, and three of his dogs were dead; their bodies were burnt. The hounds that survived suffered bruised egos and minor burns around their bodies.

He crawled outside the barrack, and his eyes met disturbed faces of slaves who were gathered outside. The commute drained what little energy he had, he could feel himself drift in and out of consciousness until his sight blurred and faded to black.

Chavez awoke to find himself in bed; "Master Chavez," he was greeted by a familiar voice. He turned slowly, his head and his eyes met with Maria who sat on the chair nearest to the bed. "You are lucky master to be alive," she said, glaring at his neck. Chavez felt a blistering pain from his neck but was too weak to lift his hand to caress it.

"The creature nearly comer (eat) you," she said, still glaring at his neck. Chavez remained silent and fixated his gaze on his cabinet. "I mopped the bruise with aloe, and I gathered the others (slaves), there was nearly a riot here, they thought you were dead," she said sweetly. "Anyway, I off to the fields, rest master," she said, slowly walking out of the room, sluggishly closing the door, gaping at Chavez until the door slammed shut.

As the door closed, Chavez slowly began counting to himself. As his lips muttered, "Treinta," he listened for Maria behind the door. He knew all too well she had a tendency to eavesdrop. When he heard her quarrelling in Creole outside through the veranda, he rolled off the bed. He fell to the hard-teak floors and heaved himself towards the white cabinet in the far corner of his room.

The cabinet's content consisted of journals and letters from his kin (grandmothers, grandfathers, mother, and father). He pulled the cabinet draw recklessly and it tumbled hard onto the floor, sending dust, parchments, and journals plummeting down and scattering in every direction. He quickly sifted through the mess and began to immerse himself in the writings. Though he sneezed and coughed hard as the dust itched his nose, this didn't hamper his yearning for any modicum of information. His thirst for knowledge was sated when he reached the writings of his mother. His eyes meticulously scrutinized her cursive writing and her rich descriptions.

He noticed a common trend in the writings about this creature. He realized that the Soucouyant was not a strange occurrence to the plantation. It appeared to each owner of the estate. His mother's account was the most in-depth, her narrative discussed the creature and her failed attempts to ward off the beast. Chavez forced himself to his feet and began to prepare, for he knew the creature would return. He beckoned a priest who he knew was staying at a neighbouring plantation. He assigned Liam's son, Lionel, to bring him promptly by horse.

"Father you took long enough!" Chavez said hastily, his patience exhausted after waiting four hours. "Yes, Chavez what is it you need?" the priest said concerned, watching Chavez's weakened appearance. Chavez walked over to the priest's bag and rudely began trawling through it, "I want that silver crucifix, the holy water, and the blessed salt; all of it," Chavez said, his hand still deep in the clergyman's bag. "What is wrong with you son, don't you have manners!" the priest said annoyed as he grabbed the bag from him. "Look I can't explain!!!" Chavez dug in his jewellery box and handed the priest gold trinkets along with a silver watch as payment. He grabbed the bag from the priest's hands, and he shoved him outside. He slammed and locked the door behind him. Chavez had recalled that the mere mention of God sent the creature running. Thus, these holy items were bound to deliver lethal blows.

Night fell over the plantation, and there was a stillness in the trees and not a cricket could be heard. Chavez perched in the veranda with the heavy crucifix well concealed under his garment, and two pounds of blessed salt, and a bottle of holy water in his pockets. He vigilantly waited for a scream but there was no sound. As the night crept on, there was no sight of the creature. Chavez grew aggravated. Then bizarrely, Lionel came at the bottom of the veranda and looked directly at Chavez. The boy muttered not a word, he merely pointed toward the edge of the plantation.

Chavez, confused at first, slowly came to understand. He limped down the stairs and outside toward the boy. He dragged himself slowly, still weak from his encounter with the beast. Chavez's eyes met with the boy's leer, his eyes bright and his face fixed. Still, Lionel uttered not a word, he just pointed toward the edge of the plantation. The man nodded and strolled in the direction Lionel pointed. He continued until he heard a strange sound of chanting. He followed the sound to the old stone building at the edge of the plantation.

This stone building was dedicated to the torturing of slaves when they were unruly, it was utilized by the prior owners. Chavez never employed such cruelty, so the building remained abandoned. The chanting grew louder as Chavez crawled carefully forward. *The language was definitely in Creole*, he thought. He entered the building and moved towards the stairs, he descended to the bottom floor. His ears recognized a voice that sounded like Maria's. When he reached the basement, he stationed himself behind a barrel, he cautiously peered and caught a glimpse of Maria and a procession of slave women. They were chanting in a circle, and there was one in the centre who looked unconscious.

She laid motionless on the ground with her eyes closed. Maria began dancing and chanting, and the girl on the ground woke up, she began screaming and steam emitted from her very skin. Her screams grew louder, whilst Maria and the other women chanted faster and rowdier to drown the woman's wailing. The steam grew thicker and her body began to contort wildly and suddenly she burst into flames. Her screams turned to the crackling of flesh. The flaming woman rose into the air, her skin melted from her bones and oozed to the floor. Chavez's eyes grew wide, quickly he grasped his mouth to muffle his gasp and urge to curse. *She was no longer human; she was a Soucouyant!* he pondered to himself in disbelief.

The flame from the beast was blood-red and at its centre, a blue silhouette of a womanly figure. The creature screeched and danced madly with anguish. "Now, go for the Master, burn him! Maria jeered wickedly. Chavez's heart sank; Maria betrayed him and his father and mother. Rage filled his body and he jumped from the shadows, "Come then monster!" he shouted in fury. Maria and the other women jerked back in astonishment. She glared at him, "So you figure out eh, it is me who set the beast on you and who turn the women into beast, but they do so willingly. Them all hate you and your family for what you do to we!!!" she said enraged.

"I never did anything, I never wanted any of this, I hate this plantation, and I never wanted to own you!!" he said with rage building in his voice. He carefully moved his hands in his pockets. Two other women in the procession began to scream, and fell to the floor, bursting into red balls of fire, leaving their skin below them. The procession ran out the back door leaving Maria and the three balls of fire to face Chavez.

"Is all the same with white skins, you all wicked and evil, now, is we turn to kill you like your family kill we. The men sacrifice themselves, don't let their sacrifice be in vain, kill him!!!" Maria signaled the three Soucouyants towards Chavez. Chavez dug in his clothes to reveal the crucifix. The creatures halted at the sight, but Maria charged in at Chavez with a knife. She swung and cut his chest, and the crucifix fastened by a chain fell to the ground. Maria grabbed the cross and wickedly grinned and the creatures charged toward Chavez.

The man clutched his chest that was bleeding profusely, and fell. His breaths were labored, and his heartbeat grew heavier and louder. The creatures encircled him, edging closer and closer to his body. Drenched in sweat, he quickly dipped in his pocket and pulled out the holy water and poured some on his head, the creatures began to slow down and flew a few feet back.

Chavez took this opportunity to charge. He threw water at the closest of the fiends. As the water met the beast, steam quickly rose from it. In agony, the beast let out a scream that shook the walls of the building. Its flame grew faint, turning into a light orange, and slowly it fell to the floor in pain. "One down two to go," Chavez said triumphantly. "You forget me!!!" Maria said as she came in again with the knife, and he rolled and dodged the blade. As he got up, one of the beasts flew by and grazed his arm.

He grunted in torment, clenching his arm in pain as it seared his flesh. The second Soucouyant came charging in for the kill. Chavez quickly bowed, but the creature grazed his back, roasting his skin. "Face it white cockroach you are going to die, give up, you going to die like all those before you for what you do to we, we go have we revenge and freedom, like Haiti we go be free!!"

Chavez glared at her, "Why Maria, you think killing me would help gain freedom, and how could you sacrifice your own people just to avoid suspicion!!!"

"Oui white man, it would, this we form of resistance, we go fight you with fire, Soucouyant fire, and them man offer themselves willingly, why you think nobody cried at the funeral!!!"

Chavez breathed deeply and said calmly, "I'm sorry Maria, but I'm not dying today," he reached for the salt and water and the two creatures came again, and the third Soucouyant recovering from the dowsing shook violently and flew up. Maria had a toothy grin and she stood back and viewed in dark ecstasy. The three beasts charged, and Chavez jumped and landed near the melted skin, some salt and water spilled and ran on the ground. The two mixed and slowly meandered and touched the melted skin near

30

him. The skin crackled and bubbled as though burning. Chavez noticed one of the Soucouyants was screaming and jerking wildly, until it grew bright, dispersed, and vanished.

Maria screamed angrily, "What did you do!!!" She raced toward him along with the two other plumes of fire. Chavez acted quickly, throwing salt to the other shambles of skin, killing the second. As he reached for the last skin, Maria kicked him and stabbed his hand. "Now dead in peace!" she shouted and stepped on his chest, and the last Soucouyant came in toward his throat.

Chavez's life flashed before his eyes, and a single tear rolled from his eye. The searing pain returned on his neck, and he bellowed in pain. The wicked grin on Maria's face grew blurred, and his sight was beginning to fade. His mind slipped into memories he had long forgotten of his father and mother; recollections of them helping him up when he tumbled as a child, flickering glimpses of them encouraging him when he failed. His heart swelled in elation as he recalled their nurturing voices echoing in his weak consciousness. But as the coldness of death began to fully engulf him, he recalled one last memory of his mother teaching him how to pray. Chavez began to pray so deeply in his mind, it managed to loosen death's grip and sustained his consciousness.

Maria, annoyed and shocked, noticed him still breathing, "I say dead in peace!!!" Maria shouted. Chavez realized that his fingers had salt and holy water residue. He mustered the strength, waved his hands weakly, and touched the beast; it flew in pain and fear. Maria angrily drew the knife and said, "I will do it myself!!!" She came closer, ready to stab him to death when Lionel came running in with the hounds, and they lunged and attacked Maria.

She screamed and bellowed as the dogs scratched and bit her. Chavez pointed to the salt on the ground and the skin. Instantly Lionel picked up the salt and dashed it on the oozing puddle of skin. The creature squealed and dispersed. Maria's screams and shrieks grew silent. Suddenly Chavez felt cold noses touching his skin. The hounds came towards Chavez and licked his wounds, he glanced over to Maria, she was maimed and mauled to death by the dogs.

A week later, Chavez had recovered somewhat from the incident and was in the veranda overlooking the plantation. A clergy of priest marched around the plantation praying religiously and dousing every patch of soil and each building with holy water. "Bonjour master Chavez," Lionel said as he came into the veranda. "You are here, I wanted to thank you for your help," Chavez said smiling. Lionel's expression was a mixture of happiness and confusion. "Master I-" before he could finish Chavez interrupted, "Just call me Chavez," he said, twisting his face in discomfort at the boy addressing him as master.

"Given everything that has happened on both sides, the sacrifices and losses to your kin and mine and my deep disgust with owning slaves, I have decided today you are free, you all are free, I will divide up the land and give each of you an acre," Chavez finished and walked towards his chair. Lionel left without saying a word, he ran happily towards the field. In the distance, Chavez heard the happy jeers, chants, and songs. He, however, knew that this act of kindness would not sit well with the local slave owners, but he was willing to take the risk.

Night fell, and the trees danced in the breeze. The air was cool and soothing, with the orchestra of crickets serenading Chavez to sleep.

4.

MERMAID POOL

He fell to his knees in frustration, clenching dirt in the palm of his hands, grinding his teeth, his breathing loud and heavy.

"Estefan calm yourself…"

"Don't tell me to be calm!" he snapped at his second in command Pablo, "We have been moving in circles, I am convinced that there is no gold on this island," he said, his face flushed crimson red with anger.

His eyes darted towards their guide Peeko. Peeko was very perturbed, as his eyes met with Estefan. He feverishly began to mop the sweat on his brow. "I implore you, as real as the air in my lungs and the blood in my veins, this is the place," Peeko said, hoping this would calm Estefan's fury.

Estefan clenched his fist so tightly that his pale bony fingers blushed red. "All I see is a pool, nothing but water!" He bellowed with such rage, spittle flew from his mouth, onto Peeko. He reached out to his guide, and quickly clenched his thin brown neck and began to squeeze, "For each day you've wasted bringing us through this hell hole of a forest, I would have them torture your family, each day worse than the last."

Peeko's face twisted and became red with discomfort. Quickly his eyes drifted to the far distance where he could see his wife and son both tied securely by Estefan's crewmen. Pablo, in dismay, quickly shifted close to his Captain, and in a concerned tone said, "Listen to yourself, threatening our guide, and after all Peeko is a Christian like yourself, how could you even fathom such a thought?"

"Peeko may be a Christian but here is where his loyalty lies, he is, after all, nothing but a savage like his family and people, he seeks to trick me, to save all the gold for himself, and for that, I would make him suffer," Estefan disgorged with bitter venom in his words. He slowly dislodged his hands from around the man's thin neck, raising them to give his men the order to kill the prisoners. Peeko wheezed and coughed profusely. He grabbed his neck and began to caress it, hoping this would ease the pain. With all the vigor his throat could allow he shouted, "Wait!" Quickly he reached for the golden nugget pendant that was fastened by a slender cloth around his neck. He moved to the lake and scanned the surface. The lake was deep blue and surrounded by black coarse stones, the water smelt fresh, and the pond was tranquil and undisturbed.

Peeko shouted with his hands raised, "Look here you would get your gold!"

Estefan looked to the water fuming. Peeko took the pendant and gently placed it in the water, letting it sink into the deep blue. As the gold pendant sank deeper into the watery abyss, he turned to his wife and mouthed to her, "Everything would be okay." His wife's eyes were red with tears, she grasped firmly unto her son as much as the cuffs could allow. In her eyes, he could see the pain, and trauma this entire ordeal had dealt. Pablo viewing the interaction moved to Estefan, "Listen, Estefan, I understand you

34

made an oath to the King and Queen to bring gold, but the pope, clergymen, the church and God himself, would not approve of this, you took a citizen of Spain, though he is a Kalinago, there was no need to kidnap his family."

"Pablo, please, save your ramblings for the clergyman, and don't you dare seek to absolve yourself of this, you in fact suggested to enlist Peeko's help to find the gold, I used his family as insurance to assure we do." Estefan spewed his words through clenched teeth, anger intertwined to each word.

He moved his gaze to Peeko as he slowly crept to the water. He stared as the golden glimmer grew dim and disappeared. Estefan waited patiently, not saying a word, hoping for some sign. Keenly he moved and kneeled at the edge of the pool, both his hands perched firmly on the stones. Straining his eyes and neck, desperately looking for a sight of maybe the bottom. *Maybe the bed was laced with gold*, he thought.

But nothing except deep blue water met his eyes, and stillness reached his ear. His nose grew hot and his head thumped as his patience expired. The man flew up in fury, charging for Peeko. He snatched a dumbfounded Peeko by the arm, his fingers gnawing into his flesh. With great force, he shoved him into the water and in a thunderous splash Peeko fell into the deep blue, and flailed wildly. Slowly, Peeko managed to settle himself in order to float. By the time his sight narrowed, he could see Estefan holding a blade to his son's throat.

His wife wailed and screamed. Her cries were interwoven with fright and melancholy. Peeko began to plead profusely, "Capitan, take me instead, I implore you, not my son."

"SHUT IT!!!" Estefan roared, "You don't understand what I stand to lose if I don't achieve this, none of you do, you sought to

35

test my patience!" He hollered, his face was swollen red and his teeth clenched tautly. Peeko's son's shoulder, shivered under his clenched fingers. So drunk with rage, Estefan couldn't hear the whimpering of the boy. "You sought to test my patience, that was your gravest mistake!" He roared and began to slowly sink the blade into the epidermis of the boy's throat.

"Please, not my son!!" Peeko screamed as he reached out, trying as best as he could to climb out of the water. The boy began to scream as the blade began to sever his skin and enter his flesh. His screams became muffled as blood streamed from the wound. Straight across the throat, Estefan dragged the knife, and he pushed the boy towards the water. The boy's body collided with Peeko's, and he fell back into the pool. Both of them sank in the water. Quickly a cloud of scarlet rose to the surface of the water, and hastily turned a deep blue cerise red. Peeko rose slowly from the water, his son clenched in his arm, crying, he dipped his head into the boy's neck as blood covered his face.

Estefan stood frozen, biting his lip, thoughts of regret pervaded in his mind, but he found all manner of excuses to justify his actions. Without thinking, Pablo made a beeline to Estefan. Mustering all the strength in his body, he pushed him, sending him face forward unto the ground. The knife flipped and splashed into the water. Pablo then grabbed Estefan by the collar of his shirt and punched him square across the face.

"Are you mad, you murdered him, a boy, in cold blood, are you crazy?"

Wiping the blood from his nose, concealing his guilt, Estefan said, "Necessary evil for the greater good."

Pablo in shock rose from the earth, and withdrew himself far from Estefan, then he turned his back and walked away from the crowd of soldiers and explorers that accompanied them. These men and women were just as hungry as Estefan was to find gold. Each temporarily hid their moral compass, hoping that the sight of gold would sate their appetite and justify Estefan's ruthlessness.

Peeko's tears mixed with blood, as he and his wife's screams of agony echoed throughout the forest. Pablo gingerly walked over to Peeko's wife and gently embraced her. She wept bitterly over his shoulder, drowning her screams on his chest. The distraught man looked up to Estefan, his once meek demeanor transformed into anger and anguish. He released his son into the water and the body gracefully sank into the deep. Peeko emerged, with both fists clenched and his eyes focused on Estefan. He slowly made his way to his enemy, when suddenly, from behind him, he heard the water roaring. Peeko and the crowd all grew silent as they witnessed the red lake twist and crash. Estefan grew fascinated as he returned to the edge of the water.

He glared at the sight, believing to himself that he caught glimpses of a human head and a large fish like tail in the midst of the water's violent trashing. "But it cannot be," he muttered to himself. Pablo, in the distance, called to Estefan, but his cries fell on deaf ears, he was entranced. Slowly, what appeared to be a woman, rose from the lake, even with her face stained red it didn't diminish her splendor. His eyes were locked as she continued walking out of the water. In her hands, was Peeko's dead son. Estefan's eyes broadened as all about the woman's brown body was freckled with scales of gold. His jaw grew loose and heavy. Peeko moved to his wife, who managed to dislodge herself from Pablo's grip. The two reached for each other and hugged tightly, with tears in their eyes. The crowd of men roared and screamed in terror, some fleeing to the woods, others falling to their knees in such fear; they wept bitterly.

"Deus animam meam!" Pablo screamed as he ebbed further from the being that emerged from the lake. He withdrew behind a tree and peered keenly from behind the thick bark. The creature's eyes were now locked on Peeko, it muttered in a language that only the couple could understand and without a moment's notice, the couple ran to the body of their dead son. Peeko took the corpse from the creature's arms and both him and his wife retreated into the forest. But before Peeko was fully out of sight, he turned for a moment and glanced at Estefan, his eyes were filled with pity and melancholy, then he quickly marched off disappearing into the woods.

Estefan, still in awe, gasped at the voluptuous body of this entity. His eyes counted each bead of gold that freckled the skin. Without thinking, he muttered, "Gold, where is it?" The creature turned its eyes to him, its deep green eyes peered deep into his as though piercing into his mind, sifting through each of his memories. Estefan suddenly began to feel a thunderous migraine. The pain was unyielding causing both of his ears to ring relentlessly. With each step the creature made towards him, the intensity of the headache grew sharper, so he clasped his bloodstained hands on his face in response to the pain.

Then, as though echoing in his brain, he heard in his own voice; "GOLD, is what you seek?" His eyes seared in pain as he fell to his side in a fetal position. He closed his eyes, and in his mind he heard his voice again in a coy tone, "Answer me, is it gold you seek?" He grunted in misery, holding his head tightly. The woman clothed in gold slowly approached and laid her cold water drenched fingers on the center of his head.

Estefan heard again in his own voice, "TELL ME IS IT GOLD YOU SEEK!!" This time, the power of the voice rattled the fabric of his mind. His eyes watered, and he cried in pain. "Yes!!" He shouted aloud, "Yes, just please stop, stop please!" The lady in gold smiled wickedly, "NO!" Estefan heard in his own deep shrewd tone. She pressed down deeper into his forehead and Estefan felt such pain that he jerked uncontrollably, until he slowly became unconscious.

"Why I wonder; why do you seek it so desperately?" The question echoed in his head, in his voice once more. The lady in Gold began to weave through his thoughts, until finally, she came to a halt, "Tell me what I want to know!" he heard in his head once more that he had no choice but to answer the beckoning call. His mind began to lead the voice to his memories. The sea of mist and darkness that was the inner workings of his mind began to materialize into the memories that the lady desired.

"Don't worry," Estefan said to his wife, stretching his arms out to hug her.

"Don't tell me not to worry, you are telling me you want to leave here to go to the new world for gold," his wife snapped back at him, forcefully slapping away his hands.

"Listen, it would be worth it, once I find enough, we won't be poor, we could afford to get Pique the medical attention he needs," he said reassuring her.

"Oh, how very noble," he heard again in his voice, booming in the background mockingly.

"But you lied, it's fame you wanted, fooling your wife into believing such folly, she is ignorant isn't she, or maybe she wanted to be drenched in gold too, that's why she didn't resist as much as she could have."

"Shut up!" Estefan shrieked in frustration.

In response, he heard; "NO," in a cool calm tone.

39

"I did this for my son, he is sick, hurts every day, but I can't afford..."

"So, you killed a son for your son, how so very selfish of you."

"I, I, I didn't mean to, I acted out of..."

"What was it, you acted out of spite, greed, the way I see it, you owe a life... wait, wait, I think we are on to something here," his voice said to him coyly.

Suddenly, he could see the lady drenched in gold before him, in the void of his thoughts. She playfully stroked her chin, she continued speaking in Estefan's voice; "You seek gold for your poor sick son and poor wrench yes, to get what you desire, pay the price, a life for a life, this is what I require."

Estefan grew speechless, he reflected on the words. His blood crawled, and his skin grew cold.

"I refuse," said Estefan.

"Of course you will refuse, you want to go home a hero, with a chest full of gold, and become a rich man, but know, your fate was decided the moment you carved open the boy's throat, but rest easy, your son would smile and your wife would get her desires."

With that, Estefan awoke, he gasped for air and his sight quickly focused and met the lady in Gold. She smiled as she sank her finger into his flesh. He jerked in torment as the finger twisted and bore deeper into his skull. From the wound, searing heat poured and coerced through his veins, traveling through every nook and crevice of his body. Pablo, who was hiding behind a tree, slowly peered as he could hear the screams of his friend. His screams grew hollow and muffled as his tongue and lungs became solid gold and from his nose and mouth rushed out golden dust.

He viewed in horror as the body of his friend grew gold and stiff. Fear left his feet glued to the earth. His last cry echoed, and made Pablo cringe in sadness. Estefan's head dipped and hit the earth hard with a deep gong much like that of a church bell. Pablo covered his mouth and bit his lips, refusing to look at the sight, instead, he shut his eyes tightly.

A stillness rose in the air, and for a moment he opened his eyes. Meekly he peered from behind the tree trunk, narrowing his eyes to see the lady. She glared at him, then turned her gaze to the body of gold and turned quickly, and returned to the water. As she withdrew, Pablo rushed forward to see his friend's body gleaming in rose gold, his expression horrific, frozen in a state of unrelenting agony. Pablo kneeled and laid his hands on the statue. It was cold, solid and heavy, he sighed, "I will get you home."

......

Screams of laughter filled the air as the once grieving wife opened a box the size of a coffin. In it pieces of a golden statue laid, broken, owing to the long commute across the sea to Spain. As she rummaged through, she discovered pieces of golden limbs piled on top of each other. She managed to grasp the head that looked so familiar to her husband's. In it, a note addressed to her and kin. Unknown to her, scribed by Pablo, *"My final gift to you my loving wife and son, may it bring you everything I've promised; a better life for all the sacrifices I've made."*

41

5.

THE RED HOWLER'S TREE

In times of old, there was a great forest. At the centre of that forest was an enormous tree that towered over the others. This tree was a marvel to the eye, its bark was golden brown, its roots were the size of horses and it formed a canopy that nearly blocked the sun's rays from touching the soil with its leaves and branches. Men never ventured into this forest, owing to fearful respect. The forest became a sacred place to the red howler monkey. They especially held in high regard the colossal tree that they made their home.

One day a great trampling sound thundered through the forest. This sound was accompanied by smoke and shouting in a language unknown to the howler monkeys' ear. Monkey scouts followed the deafening sounds to find a large group of men. They were adorned with golden headpieces neatly ornated with precious gems of red and green, accentuated with long blue feathers. Their arms and thighs dressed in golden bangles. Around saffron coloured skin, light cuirasses tightly weaved with rose-red feathers mixed with yellow cloth, along with golden armor on their shins with their feet exposed.

Their skin saffron in colour which was accentuated by the bright colours in their armor. Tightly fastened on their waist were wooden clubs and sharp stone swords which they used to clear the forest. Enraged, the howlers carelessly attacked the men, for the forest was precious to them. However, these were seasoned warriors, who easily cut them down. Disheartened, the few survivors ran back to the great tree, which was their only defence against these vile invaders.

With haste in each step, the men pursued until their eyes met the giant. Each halted their steps and were awestruck. The clan of monkeys emerged from every crevice and nook in the God-like tree. Steadily they began to screech and shout violently at the men, as they drew nearer. Unfazed by the uproar, they moved closer to the tree. The largest of the men dipped into a leathery pouch that was secured on his waist and drew a black fluid and in a quick smooth motion, he smeared it on his blade with his hand.

He then quickly took the drenched blade and ran it against the bangle on his thigh and immediately, the black blade lit into a bright yellow vicious flame. The monkeys grew silent in horror. The rest of the men followed, one by one their swords lit. One of the howlers dropped down and readied himself for the baited challenge. The largest man smiled wickedly, and stepped forward and pointed his flaming blade toward the monkey.

The howler flexed his chest and reared his fangs to invoke intimidation. The beast bellowed a cry of pride and charged at full speed towards the man. Speedily, he evaded the howler's blow and without much effort, he plunged the lit blade into the monkey's back. The beast shrieked in misery as the blade tore through its flesh. The yellow flames of the sword rumbled as it began to engulf its prey. The monkey quickly grew silent and fell to the earth; with its body charred. The sight of this shattered the howlers fighting spirit. Defeated by the sight, they knew they stood no chance and reluctantly and painfully retreated deep into the forest.

After the exodus, the men approached the tree. One inquisitive soldier walked near the golden bark and reached out slowly. He began rubbing his fingertips on the coarse bark when suddenly, it felt as though a sharp needle pierced his fingers. He withdrew his hand quickly and began scanning his tips. But his skin portrayed no sign of damage. He glared for a few seconds until he could feel pain and trauma he's never fathomed before. He then fell to his knees, clenching his arm and coughing blood.

Instantaneously he screamed, and his eyes fluttered violently until they went white. His lifeless body laid for a mere minute until his corpse ferociously began to swell and contort, and from his skin sprouted branches and leaves. Robustly, these grew into a short vibrant tree. The others viewed in terror of the tree's mystical powers.

Quickly, they returned home lamenting in terror. In the weeks that followed, troops of slaves and soldiers began a strenuous endeavour of imprisoning the tree within a narrow tall stone pyramid. This act was fuelled strictly by fear. Unfortunately, the tree shrunk under its stone pyramid prison. It was only through tiny nooks and crevices of the structure the sun rays managed to pierce through, keeping the tree just barely alive.

By design, a large rectangular space was made, large enough to expose the bark. The great tree became a form of punishment available only for the kingdom's use. Criminals and usurpers were faced with the punishment of touching the tree, doomed to become a tree themselves. Of all the unfortunate, a war criminal Picabo, was sentenced to the grim fate of touching the tree. He endured the two days' journey, without food and water, weak and

44

restless, he could no longer walk any further and he dropped to his knees.

He sighed at the bruises he had procured on his knees and his back from being dragged by taut chains that were secured around his wrist. Picabo looked around weakly, his eyes met with the pyramid and he began to forebode disaster. The soldiers screamed at him and began pulling the chain forcing his hand towards the opening. With what strength he could muster, he fought back, pulling his hand from reach. Irritated, the soldier pulled hard, in the process his hand slipped, and landed in the space touching the bark.

The soldiers shouted in shock and anger. In fear, they withdrew, ensuring a safe distance between them and their unlucky comrade. However, their eyes were glued in a strange fascination on what was about to come. The scared soldier forgot about Picabo, and was staring at his arm, his skin grew hot, and he became engulfed in sweat. His breathing grew tenfold as he began to cry hysterically. Slowly, he began to feel it; the surge of unimaginable pain. He twisted and turned uncontrollably. Under the pressure of the pain, his mind broke, and he died instantly. From the point at which his fingertips first touched the tree, branches tore through them. Tiny leaves sprouted and stood still, but for a brief moment. Once the leaves managed to get a taste of the sun's rays, the branches grew faster and more violently from the man's body. Picabo cringed as he could hear bones snap and rupture viciously.

Wasting no time, Picabo rose to his feet and with all the speed his weakened body could gather, he bolted forward to the forest. Picabo's beeline broke the guards' trance with their deceased comrade. He hastened his steps as he could hear the shouts and thuds of feet behind him. His body complained with each step forward, but he persisted manoeuvring through trunks and over roots. Suddenly his nose tickled as the smell of smoke filled the air. Picabo slowed his pace as he noticed before him was a cleared plain bordered by tall poles, drenched with crimson fire. Each was planted in the middle of deep furrows. At the base of the furrow was a stream of the black fluid, the same fluid they used on their weapons.

The flaming poles, they must be a boundary of sorts, he thought to himself. He gazed over the furrow to see nothing but thick woodlands. Behind him, he could hear the men drawing closer and closer. He inhaled deep, clenched his jaw relentlessly, and delicately took a few steps backward. He then exhaled and forced his muscles to exert the energy needed to propel him forward. The precise moment the sight of the trenches bottom became visible, he leaped. The wind rushed against his ears as he pushed himself towards the other side. He could feel the hot fumes from the black sludge rushing up towards him.

As he drew nearer to the flame pole, he twisted his frame, trying to make his body as small as possible to fit in the space between them. He closed his eyes as he drew near the flames. The fire roared viciously as he approached and he could feel the flames whip and slither as he passed by, grazing his fingers and toes.

A small price to pay, he made it through and quickly, he opened his eyes and stretched out his arms. His chest collided fiercely with the edge of the trench and with haste, he clawed his fingers in the earth and pulled himself up. Quickly, he turned around, and saw the soldiers preparing to leap across in pursuit. In desperation, one of them carelessly leaped over. Weighed down by armor and weapons, he whirled in the air until he collided with the pole of fire. His screams echoed as his body was greedily consumed by the fire. The pole owing to the force of the collision,

46

broke and fell, landing on the other side of the trench. The flame crackled and danced wildly on the pole with the impact.

A sense of relief overcame him and he smiled foolishly at his adversaries as though to taunt them. He took one last look at the jeering soldiers and trailed into the woods. The soldiers halted and watched from the other side, for they knew that his fate was going to be far worse than his sentence.

Picabo noticed the woods around him became thicker and more menacing as he proceeded further. Gradually, he began to realize the magnitude of his mistake. But he couldn't stop, he thought he had to get as far away from there as possible. He slowed his footsteps as he heard up in the trees howling that was swollen with rage. Picabo's eyes danced quickly in every direction, trying to catch a glimpse of the choir behind the howls. Focused on the chaos above him he was unaware of the thick protruding roots below him and with a large and painful thud, his foot met hard with a root and he descended to the earth face first.

"You've come... where you... should not!" a deep voice bellowed before him. Picabo rose up mopping dirt from his eyes.

"There is no home for me now, if I go back, I would be sentenced to something worse than death," Picabo said, hoping to draw pity and sympathy by his words. His eyes stung in pain as he removed the dirt from his big brown eyes. Sluggishly, the sight of a bright red blur, slowly materialized into a towering red howler monkey. Picabo quivered as he slowly began to make sense of the situation. He was surrounded by a mob of angry howlers, and the fact that one of them spoke to him in his native tongue, made his heart throb violently in his chest.

"What makes... you think you... would... be better off here!" the monkey said in a stern voice, with his face wearing an expression

47

of anger. Picabo's thoughts began to forebode all manner of torture. He shook his head as though to settle his mind and quell his thoughts. Curiosity took the better of him as he asked, "How, how is it you speak?"

"I… we have watched you… men for a long time," the monkey said, pointing his finger to his chest, then eyes.

"Since the… day you… stole our home," he said growling. Picabo quickly realized that this monkey was a chief of sorts for this troop.

"I'm not one of them," Picabo muttered, without much thought. "They raided my home and stole from us, our land and our women," Picabo paused and his eyes filled with tears, sadness overtook him as his mind reflected on the ordeal.

"Similar," said the monkey pointing to his chest, then to Picabo, inquisitively looking at him.

Picabo noticed the subtle difficulties in the beast's command of the tongue, the creature would pause, earnestly sewing together the correct words.

"Murdered, beat and defiled… my home and used it to… torture their enemies!" The beast spewed his words bitterly.

Picabo remained silent, he could sense the violence in the monkey's voice. As he spoke, Picabo felt and heard the clan of monkeys grow unsettled and livid. His words were like embers growing into a flame in his people. *I face death on both fronts, by a tree or by these howlers*, Picabo thought to himself.

"We kill… only if you provoked," the monkey said, as he could smell the fear of death on Picabo.

"No, no provoke!" Picabo stuttered in fear and relief.

The chief nodded in approval, then muttered, "Rest," then pointed to the food and motioned his hands to show eating.

Picabo was speechless, he blinked stupidly in disbelief. Quickly at his feet ripe fruits were brought to him, each howler gesturing him to eat quickly. His stomach churned and groaned with the sight of the ripe mangoes, pawpaw and avocadoes before him. With chains still binding him, he bowed his head and bit into the mangoes first. Tears wilted in his eyes as the sweet flesh and skin of the fruit reached into his palette. Eager to quell his complaining stomach, he swallowed without much chewing.

Behind him approached a young howler, grasping a sharp stone. Unaware, Picabo didn't realize the beast was behind him until he heard the loud clank, and felt a sudden release in tension around his arms. Startled, he rolled and flew to his feet, mango flesh smeared all over his face. The echoes of laughter filled the forest. Consumed with shame, Picabo wiped his face, while smirking at the trees and the tiny howler.

After making quick work of the meal, the chief slowly approached him and sat face to face. His red coat shone brightly in the evening rays, that managed to pierce through the thick forest canopy. He remained quiet with his brown eyes fixed on Picabo and his left hand slowly running through his beard. Uncomfortable by the chief's unblinking gaze, Picabo cast his eyes to his bruised fingers. The chief's eyes slowly glided from the man's head to his feet, then they came to a sudden halt at the sight of Picabo's burnt toes.

"You fear?" The monkey said while pointing to the burns. Picabo looked and thought for a moment.

He raised his eyes and looked to the monkey then observed the burns he acquired, and calmly stated, "Yes."

The monkey sighed, raising both arms and looking to his kin he said, "This, this, is not home, feathered ones took it from us and misused it," pointing to Picabo's arms to indicate fire, "Use to keep us away," he continued.

"Look," he said to Picabo, the chief took his finger and began to draw in the dirt. Slowly and carefully he drew a great tree and within its branches, monkeys. To the top of the tree, he drew a monkey larger than the rest.

He looked up at Picabo and said, "My great grandfather, the tree was home, a source of life, from it we draw food and life, and in turn, we guard and protect it."

He pointed to the tree, "Home passed down for generations, from him." He used his other finger and pointed to the monkey at the top, "To him, to him and to me," he said, slowly taking his hands and tapping his chest. "My duty is to look over it and pass it down to my kin."

Picabo noticed the subtle shift in emotion and melancholy expression on the monkey's dark, worn face. He remained silent and noticed that all around him the monkeys bore expressions of pain and sorrow. Each looking uncomfortably perched in the trees. Picabo sighed heavily and began to remember his own home and how the foreign soldiers burnt it to the ground.

Picabo covered his face as though to suppress his memories. Slowly he removed his palms from his face and said, "I will help you."

The chief closed his eyes, smiled, and took a breath to contain his elation. He took his hands and planted them firmly into the ground and quickly on his eyes and said, "Thank you." For two weeks the chief, Picabo and his best fighters planned incessantly about the foreboding attack. Each sharing tales of their history and knowledge along the way. All had mutually agreed that Picabo was the key to winning the fight ahead.

Over that time, Picabo's eyes tirelessly viewed countless carved earth detailed schematics of the planned choice of attack. Each day, Picabo and the Chief traversed the periphery forest, noting carefully, details of the land and the pyramid prison encasing the tree. More specifically, the once fiery pole that stood ever-burning now laid horizontally. The scorched pole touched either end of the trench, which could act as a bridge to either side. Also, scaffolding was installed near the peak of the tree's prison for repairs.

It was the hottest day of the week, and the earth was starved of any cool breeze to soothe the blistering heat. The soldiers that were on duty were too distracted by the weather and was unaware of a sneaking Picabo emerging from the forest. Quietly, he crept, ensuring to use the cover of the tall shrubs and tree trunks to conceal his presence, and he quickly made a beeline toward the pyramid's base and waited.

Vigilantly, he looked to see if any guard caught wind of him. Satisfied, he realized that his cover was still concealed. He drew a deep breath and raised both hands over his mouth. He quickly cupped both hands on either side of his mouth, and with all the strength that his throat could allow let out a bellowing rally cry.

This howl thundered all the way to the periphery of the forest. The sun scalded guards quickly transitioned, startled to high alert, each following the sound. Picabo, once he had finished, ensured the pouch around his waist was fastened, and quickly he began to scale the pyramid as his eyes set on the scaffolding near the peak.

Beneath him, he could hear the howlers rallying cry. Hundreds of monkeys were pressing from the forest, sticks and stones in hand, attacking any soldier in their sight. The plan was to overpower the soldiers before they could ignite their swords. The enemy soldiers that pursued Picabo, retreated to the bottom to join the fray against the howlers, while the chief pressed forward with haste to the pyramid. He climbed quietly shadowing Picabo's path.

As Picabo's fingers touched the wooden scaffolding platform, he could hear the clambering of feet towards him. Quickly he ascended to the top and his eyes met with four soldiers, already with their swords lit. Each lit with blue flames, roaring in hunger for Picabo's flesh. He fished quickly from his pouch, a sharp stone. The stone was fashioned and given to him by the chief. Before the soldiers could reach closer to Picabo, he plunged his weapon into the stone pyramid, leaving a crack in the wall. Instantaneously the sun rays rushed into the crevice and landed on the dormant branch. The rays had merely caressed the tree for mere minutes when suddenly, the branch forcefully burst through the crack and collided violently with the soldiers that were nearest. With the collision, they flew off the platform and plummeted to the ground. Their screams turned to chokes as before they met the earth, their bodies contorted and mangled as branches erupted from their limbs. The trees rained down unto the battlefield, crushing soldiers under their trunks and branches.

The sacred tree continued to disgorge from its derelict prison, branches emerged rapidly, voraciously consuming the sunlight which it had been deprived of for so long.

Picabo fought hard to maintain his footing as the scaffolding shifted rapidly and the pyramid began to rupture. Below him he could hear the foundation of the scaffolding snap as a branch collided with it. To further worsen his plight, branches slithered towards him at full speed. His memory, ripe with what would happen if the tree made contact with him, forced him in desperation to leap off the platform and scale upward to the peak. The soldiers below ogled in horror at the tree emerging in a tumultuous fashion. In stark contrast, the monkeys swelled in pride and a vigor ignited within them, filling them with grit and courage.

The earth shook, and Picabo could hear loud cracks emitting from the pyramid. He quickly continued until he reached the top. He put the sharp tool in his mouth, fastened both arms tightly around the peak, and through his nose he drew in a deep breath of air, and with his stronger hand took the tool, and quickly began thrusting it into the stone peak. With each strike, he could feel the stone prison grow weaker and weaker until the tool stuck. He pulled as hard as he could, but the tool remained lunged.

He kissed his teeth and cursed, in frustration, "Hurry up and move!" He shouted. Then as though in response, he heard a large and thunderous creek that frightened him. The once rigid peak trembled below the tool, and the long crack began to slither downward hastily. Through the cracks, branches crept through with vigor, eager to escape to taste the sun and air. Picabo began to sweat profusely. He looked below him to measure the distance, but his eyes met with netting branches that were incessantly stretching and growing.

Then suddenly, from the summit of the peak, the crown of the tree leaped up; stretching up in ecstasy to the sky, obliterating the summit, and sending Picabo plummeting down with a hailstorm of rocks behind him. Picabo screamed in fear, floundering his arms wildly as the earth and branches quickly approached before him, and the raining stones quickly loomed behind him.

The tree grew upward as though reaching for the stars and then froze, its height towered over all the land. As its roots began to spread and stretch above and below ground, earthquakes came in its wake. The number of soldiers quickly dwindled as they came into contact with either the vengeful tree roots or branches. The monkeys quickly darted to the tree to avoid the tremors.

Picabo grew hoarse from his screaming, his body was soon to collide with a thick branch, so, he closed his eyes and began to pray. The Chief was in awe at the tree, and his focus broke when he heard the screams of Picabo rushing down towards him. The monkey quickly sprung to action, patiently he waited until Picabo drew closer. He dug his feet into the branch, garnering strength, and at the precise moment, he leaped, grabbed on to him, and carefully placed him on his shoulder.

After he secured Picabo in his long fury arms, he noticed the stones plummeting down. He leaped from branch to branch carefully trying to avoid making contact with the tree for fear of killing Picabo. Picabo, still trying to catch his breath from the ordeal, noticed that the branches were still stretching all around them. He huddled and curled trying to make himself as small as possible on the shoulder of the howler, trying to evade any livid branch that may want to whip him.

The chief managed to land on one of the lower branches nearest to the ground, and he viewed the landscape around him. "Oye look," he said to Picabo as he turned around for the terrified man to view the sight. The man's jaw dropped as he saw the entire area was now engulfed in evergreen. Vegetation stretched as far as the eye could see. What was once soldiers and men were now emerald canopies of trees. Scores of howlers echoed through the air as the monkeys danced and praised, nestled and perched in the sacred tree.

Picabo's eyes widened as he could see the civilization of men was now buried and under thick vegetation. The trees' roots spread far to ensure it sated its vengeance.

Once the quakes had settled, the chief scaled down to the earth and placed Picabo firmly on the ground. The man turned to view the earth, now littered with broken blades and freshly rooted twisted trees.

The chief simply touched his chest and muttered gratefully, "Thank you, grateful," while bowing his head. He then pointed to the tree and said, "You are forever welcomed."

He firmly placed his hand on the tree and grasped the arm of Picabo. He ushered the man's hand towards the tree. Picabo winced and pulled trying to move from the chief's grip. "What are you doing, after I did all this for you, how!!"

The chief looked at him ready to reprimand him, "Noo, Noo," he said, as he placed Picabo's hand on the tree.

Picabo shouted and screamed in fear and anger. But all he could feel was the warmth of the bark, he felt no pain or crackling of his bones, just warmth.

The chief looked at him, "It is grateful also," he said, releasing Picabo from his grip and he scaled up the tree swiftly.

Picabo stood still, his hand glued to the bark. In awe and looking up at the magnificent tree before him, he muttered, "You're welcome."

6.

GRANDPA'S WATER

"**I** am fed up, maybe some discipline from Gramps would do him good," the woman said, her cheeks scarlet in annoyance.

"But honey, I don't think he could handle a sixteen-year-old around his house," the man replied, pleading to his enraged wife.

"Listen, my gramps could more than manage, this imbecile that I have for a son, he doesn't seem to understand, so it's better he goes far away before I end up in a cell."

"Honey!" the man rebutted with a stroke of annoyance in his tone, that his wife swiftly identified.

She batted a menacing glare, that quickly coaxed him to readjust his pitch. "Honey, the man is two hundred years old."

She screwed her face, "Would you stop embellishing, he is old yes but far from senile or weak, and this is already decided so could we go please, Eli, car, now!" she said, pointing her sharp index finger toward the car.

Eli, though always eager to test his mother, reluctantly followed and chose to forego an argument. He slowly got in and kept his face glued to the window, to avoid any lethal glares from his mother through the rear-view mirror. A mixture of shame and anger bubbled in him as he reflected on his impending court case.

He sighed loudly as he reflected, and the thought of consequences, worried him. He mopped his brows and rose his eyes to meet the stares of the belligerent woman. Quickly his sight turned to view the thick emerald green forest along the wide meandering road.

The boy grew bored of the silence and the view of the long droning widening roads, and green blurs. After three hours, his mother had finally begun to slow the car's pace, they had finally reached her grandfather's house. The car brakes screeched loudly, sighing in relief that the long journey had reached its end. Eli's head felt heavy; the long drive made him feel uneasy. He massaged his temples as he stepped out of the car. His eyes came across the wide spanned field that was surrounded by a short grey stoned fence and he turned to see the house, white and fashioned in old colonial architecture. Sugar white and decorated with potted plants on the veranda, all filled with herbs and spices of every kind, native to the island.

"That smell of seasoning never gets old," Eli's mother said, as she stepped out of the car. She slowly walked to the door, then she heard a cool gentle voice say, "I thought you weren't coming again, I got bored and took a walk to the stream." Eli looked over to see a tall, skinny man, with a cloud of white hair. His face was salted with short white hair around the chin and cheek. His face was littered with liver spots and he exuded an air of kindness about himself. His face had wrinkles mostly around his mouth, due to years of smiling.

"Pa!!" she said, with a smile stretched across her face and arms wide rushing to embrace him.

The man's face grew red as they hugged, his frail body looked rather limp pressed against the woman's, his skinny arms barely covering much space on the woman's back.

"Pleasant Good day sir, how are you?" Eli's father said as he trailed closer to the veranda.

He released the woman and turned to the man, "I am fine- all is well?"

"All is... not that well," he responded, turning to Eli.

"Ah Eli, you have gotten so much taller, you're practically a man," the man said, a smile glued to his wrinkled face.

Eli merely shrugged at the response; he uttered no words.

Pa stood eyeing the boy waiting for a gesture of manners.

"Hello Eli, where are your manners?" his mother jeered, her eyes narrowed in anguish.

"Afternoon," he said, under his breath looking away to the field.

Pa turned away and looked to the woman, "Well, come in, come in, there is food in the refrigerator, it's just for you to warm it up, come, come!" he said, waving his hands, gesturing them to come in.

Eli remained silent for well over an hour, he avoided eye contact, to ensure he would not ignite any unwanted conversations with Pa. His mother made an extra effort not to look at him while enjoying the nostalgic talks with Pa. It was as though the sight of him would remind her of the pain and vexation.

"Well, I think it's time we get going hun," Eli's father said, as he tapped the face of his watch.

"Already, but we just got here," she said with a frown on her face, she got up and moved to the window, drawing the curtain to see how dark it was outside.

"Oh yeah, it's getting late and there are no streetlights along the road here, why you don't have them come and put them up Pa?" she said, tilting her head watching him.

"I have to remember to call them, the memory's not as good as it used to be," he said, with a smile stretched across his time-worn face.

"I will call and remind you," she said, moving towards him to embrace him with a hug.

Eli looked over and could hear his mother whispering, her words sounded like gentle whistles. He coaxed his ear, and could hear the words, "Please... I don't know what to do again... help him."

Eli's father approached him breaking his concentration. He merely looked at him and laid his hand on his shoulder. They spoke not a word, but he knew his father would want him to behave and comply. After the moment of silence, he turned from Eli, walked over to Pa and pat him on the back, and left the house. His mother then followed. Before she exited the door, she looked over to Eli, mopping her eyes, "Listen, and behave!" she said sternly and walked to the car.

Eli could hear their footsteps, each step melancholy and heavy. There was a long-drawn silence before the car engine rattled and started. "Are they having second thoughts, I wonder?" Pa said playfully as he noticed their delay to depart. Then the creaking sound of tires meeting the pitch followed and Eli quickly moved to the window. He sombrely watched as the car grew minuscule in the distance, then slowly disappeared.

"Eli, let me show you to your room, you would be here for about a month, right?"

Eli simply nodded in agreement. He grabbed his large duffle bag, and slowly followed as his great-great-grandfather walked him around the house indicating rooms. Eli hid his astonishment at the magnificence of the house, and the detailed wooden old colonial architecture. The house was old but was very well maintained.

"This is your room, you like it, I gave you the room with the best view!" he said smiling.

Eli's eyes quickly scanned through the room, noticing the huge comfortable bed, the big television, closet, and access to his own bathroom. He smirked and nodded in approval.

"I refurnished it myself, so you would at least be comfortable," the old man smiled, revealing even more etched wrinkles on his face.

Eli, for the first time in weeks, muttered, "Thank you," his lips and tongue felt strange, these words were alien to him as though he was speaking a different language.

The old man, in approval, tapped his shoulder and smiled, "Well Elias, I'm off to bed, I'm not as young as I used to be, you, you know where everything is?" he asked raising his chin.

"Yes, I do, good night," he said, chewing his words; talking under his breath in a low tone.

"Okay Eli, rest well." With that, the man retreated briskly to his room. Eli could hear the door slam and locked tightly as he reached his haven.

The boy then turned to his room, jumped onto his bed, and laid. Sleep never visited him as he stared for hours, filled with regret.

He reflected on his poor decisions and his long list of mistakes that led him to this point. The point where he could no longer elude consequence.

Before he knew it, he could hear the cock crowing outside and the sun's rays were eagerly peering through his window.

"Did you manage to get any sleep?"

Eli flew up, he hadn't noticed the old man by his door.

Eli shook his head indicating no to him.

"Strange, me either; I had a lot on my mind."

Of course, you would, Eli thought, *you are a very old man after all*, he chuckled to himself.

"But I am old after all, all the memories in here," he said, pointing to his bald spot on the centre of his head laughing.

Eli covered his mouth to contain his laughter.

The boy noticed the old man was scratching a rather red spot on his arm.

"Come, come go brush your teeth, it's time for us to go eat," the old man said ushering him downstairs.

After a full breakfast of homemade bread, scrambled eggs, garnished with sticks of turkey bacon, and tall glasses of freshly squeezed grapefruit juice, the two sat massaging their bellies.

"Was it good?" the old man asked.

"Mm hmm," Eli replied, rubbing his belly.

Again, the man could not resist the urge to itch profusely, so much so the boy could no longer ignore, "What's wrong?"

"Hmm, oh the itching, damn mosquitoes last night had a feast on my old carcass," he said kissing his teeth in frustration.

"But anyway, was it good?"

"Good," Eli responded.

"Good, Now Eli," he said, his cool tone now shifting into something more serious and focused.

"Your mother asked me to keep an eye on you, she asked if you could stay here for some time. Now, she didn't tell me what's wrong, but feel free, to tell me when you're ready," he paused, now sitting up and narrowing his focus on the boy.

"Now, I know a man must have secrets and I understand that, if you don't want to tell me what's going on, I understand."

"I robbed someone," Eli said quickly, not allowing the man to finish his speech.

"Well, I didn't expect you to talk too quickly, I thought at least three more meals," he said, rubbing his chin in wonder.

"I robbed them then beat them on school property."

The man sighed, "Why would…"

"I did it because the guy upset me, he nagged and insulted me for the entire semester, so I lashed out, I pummelled him and left him unconscious in the cafeteria, took his wallet too."

Pa rubbed his forehead uneasily, "Eli, there was no need for that, violence isn't the way, we've had this conversation."

"I know, I know."

"Then if you know, why do you resort to it constantly boy, we talked about this at least five times, this time may be the one that gets you."

"You don't have to finish Pops," Eli retorted in annoyance, "Look, I get it, but people annoy me, they pick on me, I try Pa; I really do but they won't leave me be."

"And I'm sure each of those times you were completely innocent?" Pa asked in a sarcastic tone.

Eli shrugged his shoulders and avoided making eye contact with the old man.

"Listen, I want you to be aware that all actions have…" he paused as though the words were too heavy and painful for his lips and tongue to say, then uttered, "All actions have consequences."

He paused again mopping his head, "Listen, we would talk more on this later, come on, I need help in the yard, go to my study and get the bag of bearing salt, it's in a small white bag near my desk," he said, gesturing his thin bony fingers in the direction of his room.

Eli simply dipped his head and proceeded slowly towards the room. As the boy pushed open the door he was greeted by the smell of frankincense. He slowly walked, his eyes drifting swiftly around as though he expected something to pounce out at him. He carefully planted his feet on the varnished wooden floor and glared at the tall cupboards of books, the odd trinkets hanging on the wall, and the old maps and globes on the desk. As he peered closer on the desk, he noticed a clear plastic container of water, the water was swarmed with mosquitoes. He quickly flung his hand chasing them away, and quickly, closed up the windows. "Damn pest," he said, kissing his teeth. As he peered closer in the water, he noticed the water was infested with larvae.

63

"This is why gramps scratching so much," he said. He took up the plastic container, reopened the window, and quickly threw the water out.

Just then he heard, "Eli, where are you!"

He winced as he heard the old man's voice booming through the house and responded,

"Coming now!"

He frantically dropped the container, grabbed the bag of salt, and ran downstairs.

....

Everything hurt, as both of them dragged their fatigued bodies into the house. "I am so tired I could barely move," the old man said.

Eli twisted his face, "Tired, you barely did as much as me, all you did was give me orders," he said snidely.

The old man laughed, "You know what to do now, so tomorrow, there 'would be less to order."

The old man let out a loud roar as he stretched, hoping that it would relieve his back pain.

He massaged his back, "This pain is reminding me of my age," he said, as he screwed his face. "I'm going in boy, there is food in the refrigerator, remember to call your mother okay," he said, as he moved sluggishly towards the stairs, and towards his room. Eli sat and sighed, the thought of calling his mother made him feel uneasy, but he had to, not doing so would mean an argument at a later date.

As he moved towards the phone, he heard a ferocious clamor. Eli jerked in confusion, "Old man, you okay?"

The outburst continued livid and bitter, followed by thrashing. Eli stopped and carefully moved towards the stairs, "Old man!!" he shouted as his apprehension increased. The old man's door flew open and slammed hard against the wall. Eli could hear the old man's steps smashing in rage on the wooden floor. Eli stopped at the foot of the stairs and waited. "Boy!!" the man screamed in such rage that Eli skipped back.

Eli could see the man with the plastic container clenched so taut in his hands, his skeletal fingers were red.

"The water in this, what did you do with it, did you drink it!!"

As the old man slowly climbed down the stairs, Eli stood flabbergasted, the old man's features were transformed, his wrinkled face was red with anger, his nose flared, eyes glistened with tears of anger, and his teeth clenched and bared.

"Answer me!!" he roared, in a voice that shook the drums of Eli's ears. The old man's tone began to annoy Eli.

"Calm down old man!" Eli responded.

"Who the hell you think you snapping at?" The man drew back and threw the container, hitting Eli square in the head.

Eli in shock inched back, nursing his head with his hand.

"I didn't drink it, I threw it out, there were mosquitoes in the water," he responded cool and calm, his head bowed.

"You what, you what, you have any idea what you…?" Rage grasped the old man, so tightly he could barely speak, he began to erratically rub his face with both palms. He moved them to his balding head and looked to the ceiling, then he dropped down and sat on the stairs.

A dazed look came over his face. He propped both hands on his knees, and sat silent, Eli looked at him confused. He wanted to ask if he would be okay, but the rage owing to his bruised forehead wouldn't allow him.

A single tear tumbled down the old man's liver-spotted cheek.

"I…" Eli said.

"Don't bother to say anything it doesn't matter," the old man replied.

"But the water," said Eli.

"Don't, it doesn't matter now, you wouldn't have known." The old man said with sorrow in his tone.

"Known what?" asked Eli.

The old man sighed, he mopped a few more tears that rolled down his face, he looked up to see blood flowing through Eli's fingers. The impact of the container's rim on Eli's head caused a minor wound.

"You're bleeding, shit you're bleeding," the old man got up and quickly went into his room. Eli could hear him violently rummaging through drawers. Swiftly, the man came out with a bandage, handing it to Eli. Eli looked to the old man, walked off, opened the door, and went to the veranda.

He found a comfortable spot on the stairs and muttered in anger and rage to himself. The old man slowly pursued,

"I understand your rage, tomorrow I would call your mother, and tell her to take you home."

"I was trying to help you, old man, I saw you scratching and there were mosquitoes breeding in that damn stale water!" he said, turning to watch the old man.

"I owe you an explanation, but first and foremost, sorry," he said, and stretched out his hand with the bandage.

Eli again ignored his gesture; his eyes were stern and fixed on the old man's wrinkled face. Teeming with regret, he sighed loudly and slowly withdrew his hand. The setting sun cast a long shadow upon him. This made his once warm features, dissipate. He looked much more distraught and gaunter.

"The water is much more valuable than any gold or money this world has to offer."

He paused again sticking his long bony finger into the container, hoping to scrape some residue of the liquid.

"I tell you, had you known its weight boy, then a few mosquitoes in it would mean nothing."

Eli twisted his face at this, "Then tell me was it worth this, my mistake?" the boy said, as he swiftly removed his hand revealing the bleeding wound, his tone drenched with anger much like the blood in his fingers.

The old man again stretched his hand with the bandage to the boy, still hoping the boy would take it.

Eli ignored and turned his face looking at the sun slowly creep away behind the trees in the distance.

"For you to understand, I must start from the beginning, I know I am not in any position to demand anything from you but I ask two things, one, never tell anyone of this, and that after, you accept my apology," he said in a stern tone.

Eli refused to say anything, but he noted the subtle difference in the old man's voice and intonation, he had never heard him so serious or cold before.

"Understand what I'm about tell you I have never told anyone, not even your mother, and she is my eyeball," he said, as he breathed in deeply as though he was heaving the words from his gut with much difficulty.

The old man closed his eyes fishing through his memories. He twisted his face and clasped his eyes tautly as though he was in pain or embarrassed by the thoughts, "Imagine me, boy," he muttered, his eyes still shut.

"Imagine me younger, less stoic, reckless, foul mouth, and foolish, all qualities that put me in a jail cell. Back then, cells weren't as well kept as they are now, not that I know what it looks like now, but being there got me smallpox."

Eli tilted his head, "What is that?"

"Not important, just listen," the old man said, his eyes still shut, his finger flirting with the rim of the container, hoping for some semblance of water.

"I stayed there and suffered; it was there for the first time in my life I began to mutter a prayer to God. And strange enough, for a fool like me, he answered in the most unlikely way. I could never forget the jailer's expression as he approached me with his fat greasy face, telling me that I was getting out to serve the rest of my sentence on a ship to the new world. He made sure to teasingly say I would die, either on the way or by the cannibals that lived there."

He paused, he chuckled, a smile stretched across his face, and continued his account, "Of course, being as hasty as I was, I told him it was better than the last thing I see was his fat ass, I lost some teeth over that comment, but not before those teeth took a chunk of his ear."

Eli jerked his head backward, the thought of this old man engaging in such language and violence was difficult to fathom.

"But I managed to get out of that dreary cell into another prison, this time I was bound to wood and sea instead of bars. The ship was called," he paused, rubbing his chin taxing his time-worn brain for the answer, but to no avail, he couldn't remember. He merely shrugged and continued;

"Nothing boy and I tell you nothing is as terrifying as the sea, but it was much better than staring at four dirty walls. I spent most of the day vomiting and fighting. At nights I was terrified at how dark it was, drinking myself to sleep to numb the fear and pain of the smallpox. In drunkenness and desperation, I would drench the areas where the blisters were the worst, in alcohol. My screams would wake up the crew, many times this frustrated them to the point of bitter scuffles."

The old man stopped and began to rub his feet and legs as he remembered the torment he had gone through. "Eli, our numbers dwindled along the way, a lot of corpses I threw overboard myself, and just when I thought I was going to be another corpse on the deck, we had finally made it to this island. You see, we settled on this island, in fact, not too far from this very spot," he said stamping his feet on the wooden step. "But I am getting ahead of myself. When we landed, our destination was a small village where we and the locals would interface, boy I tell you along the way I was gaping and amazed at what I saw."

69

He turned to Eli and smiled and began motioning his hands to describe; "I had never seen such green hills and crystal clear streams, the place was hot and rugged, and there was all manner of creatures my mind had never known existed," he said, enthused looking to Eli, who didn't share his sentiments.

"We sailed from the coast all the way up along meandering rivers, hugged tautly by thick canopies of trees and bamboo, and serenaded by wild birds and resilient mosquitoes, much bigger than those that you saw today, I'm sure. Then we finally came to a halt at a make-shift town, that housed Portuguese and the people of this strange place. But everyone here didn't share my awe, maybe lengthy time here stripped it away from them. The Portuguese were all sun-baked and crusted, spewing all manner of curses at the natives, coaxing them to do their bidding, either it was about gold, agriculture or infrastructure works," Pa said with much discomfort.

"I knew disdain when I saw it, these native people were not happy, I could see their disgust towards my kin, and seeing that there were more of us made it worst."

"Why didn't they like you, old man?" Eli asked.

"It's complicated, but looking back on everything Eli, it was justified, but there was only one of them that emitted a sense of happiness and kindness towards us, towards me, Ayma."

"Ayymaa," Eli said, trying hard to pronounce the name correctly.

"She was beautiful, had long flowing hair, brown silky caramel skin, she was unlike anything I had ever seen."

"What this has to do with the water?" Eli interjected.

"Boy you're too impatient, I am getting to that," the old man said as he sighed."

"You young people like to hustle everything. We were assigned to scour the land for gold or spices; anything of value that could be taken back home. But you see, that search had led my people to do desperate things, and treat these people in ways I'm too ashamed to mention," the man said as he sighed heavily, looking down at his feet in shame.

"For weeks we engaged in expeditions in search of gold, and each time we came up short the people there were treated poorly. I too, in frustration did some things, those expeditions were the worst and this place was hot and my illness became exacerbated as the days progressed."

Eli looked at him, "But you survived, how?"

"Every night I was placed in a thatched roof house with others who had pox as well, a lot of them were in far worse shape than myself, some either went to sleep and never woke up or died on the expedition. Eli, laying with them made me feel as though I was flirting with death, and I had plans to live, so I would go and sleep on the outside, on the veranda."

"Yeah, but how did you get healing," Eli said in frustration.

The old man kissed his teeth and continued, "Remember that girl, Ayma, she came to me one night, with a calabash bowl of water, washed my feet, I had never once spoken to her, but I guess maybe on one of the trips up the rivers looking for gold, she felt pity for me. The gesture of kindness, I was not accustomed too, I couldn't even bring myself to say thank you, but before long my toes winced and burned and suddenly boy before my eyes, boy as true as there is a God in the sky, the pox disappeared," the man said in such excitement that Eli's pores rose.

"What!" Eli said in disbelief.

"Yeah, Eli as true as there is air and the sun in the sky, it was healed." Eli turned and eyed the man sternly.

"I don't like being lied too," Eli said, his face shifting into an expression of anger.

The man held his gaze, his grey eyes unwavering, "You said that there were mosquito larvae in the water not so?" he said, his tone stern and assured.

"Go to the back, see what became of them, and if you manage to find the concrete damp with water, take some and put it on the wound."

Eli kissed his teeth and said, "No!"

"Fine then, I would go myself, follow if you want." The old man slowly rose and reached for a lantern he had sitting on the veranda floor. He quickly lit it and slowly climbed down the stairs an advanced to the back of the house. The lantern firm in one hand, and the bandage fixed in the other.

Eli sat, and tapped his legs uneasily until his patience failed him, and curiosity overtook him, he quickly got up and followed. Outside was pitch black and filled with the sounds of all manner of insects and birds belonging to the night, but no mind Eli paid to any of this, his eyes stayed glued to the ground hoping to see the drying splashes of water or dead larvae.

Finally, his eyes met the site, but there were specks, moving slowly. The old man stopped and pushed the lantern forward to better illuminate the area. Eli slowly got down to his knees and hunched as low as his body could allow.

"I, what!" he gasped, as he saw the tiny pupae, twisting and twitching with life, he rubbed his eyes as though they were deceiving him.

72

He exclaimed, "But it has been over hours, the water is gone but they are!"

"Alive, I told you," said the man.

"But how, why, they should be,"

"Dead? I know, but they are not dead, the water is in their bodies, it would sustain them, heal them until…" said Pa. Eli turned and sat on the ground in dismay, he then turned to the man in horror and astonishment, and asked, "You, how long?"

"Longer than I could remember, but the last of it was what you threw." Pa answered.

Eli's eyes welled up, owing to a thick mixture of sorrow and empathy. "I am, I didn't…"

"It's okay boy, you wouldn't have known."

Eli reached out his hands towards the man, beckoning the bandage without a word. There was a long cool silence as Eli placed the white bandage on his wound. Slowly he began to process the gravity of all that laid before him.

"How old are you- wait how long have you been here, how did- I have so many questions."

"Am sure you do Eli, feel free, I owe you that much."

Eli composed himself, clasped his hands, and dipped his head between his index fingers and thumbs.

"Tell me what else happened," he said, as he slowly raised his head looking at the old man.

The old man smiled, "It's a shame, you could have gotten some to put on the wound."

"Tell me the rest, where did Aaymi get the water from?"

"Ayma boy, her name is Ayma," he said as he slowly perched on the ground near Eli.

"Much like how you feel now, I was ecstatic by this, and went to the leaders, and urged them about the water and lamented on its value, of course, like you, they needed evidence. So, I managed to muster all the smallpox patients and half of the abled bodied men and sought out Ayma, who agreed with great elation. Boy, she took us further than I have ever seen, far beyond the village, up to a mountain of evergreen trees. We crossed many wandering tributaries of crystal-clear waters. Until we finally got to a pool of water that glowed blue. The water had a strange stillness, and there were no fish or any other animal drawn to it," he said, with a strange sense of awe as though the sight was before his grey eyes.

"Ayma had with such care ushered all the sick into the water, and one by one boy we were healed, such kindness I had never known, boy I remember the smiles on all of their faces, and the anxiousness to get back to recount such a tale, boy, of course, I took a bath and voraciously drank the water."

The old man paused, and his face grew grim, his breaths became heavier.

"Old man, are you okay? Eli asked concerned.

The man took his cool time to answer, "I am … fine."

"What happened?" Eli asked, anxious to hear the rest of the story.

He took a deep breath and continued, "Eli, sorry, where was I, yes, as we neared the village the scent of smoke filled the air, a few of the men and the woman in the group grew uneasy and ran

74

to the village, Eli boy when I got there, I saw fire and smoke, everything was either burnt to ash or dead."

"What, I don't understand, what happened," Eli said concerned.

"Boy, the natives, they had revolted and were winning. Etched in my mind, were maimed bodies both of my kin and the natives. Those that weren't dead were either scampering for safety or fighting with horrific fervor."

Eli's face was distraught, "And Ayma, was she okay?"

"When I saw the fire, boy something in me stirred, and brewed into a bitter rage, I forgot about kindness, I forgot about good deeds and healing, my feeble mind believed that Ayma was part of this, she had to have agreed to this to divide our numbers I thought, she had to, had to, I..."

The man gasped for air as his voice began to break.

Tears descended from his eyes as he continued, "I, cursed her and accused her of all that happened, her face is forever in my mind, fear mixed with sadness, I clenched her shoulders, shook her with such rage, her face and body grew red, but she managed to fight me off, one solid kick in the stones crippled me as she disappeared in the chaos."

He stopped once more to compose himself, Eli looked on not saying a word, his face veering with sadness and disgust.

"But the fire in me grew even fiercer I was not going to give up, I picked up a blade from a dead comrade and pursued into the chaos. Left and right those around me were dying, well-placed arrows and spears ensured their swift death. They served as shields for me as I pursued, stabbing, maiming and killing attackers along the way." He stopped, covered his face, and began to weep bitterly.

He sniffed violently, trying to compose himself, he continued, sadness leaking from his voice; "With each dead comrade I saw, I clenched the sword tighter, but swiftly I was humbled, and surrounded by livid warriors, their bodies festooned with blood and ash, their weapons baptized in blood, these men were relentless, and with each hit and cleave they landed I felt the strength leave my body until I fell to my knees, but somehow Eli, before my eyes grew too heavy to lift, a foreign strength swelled in me and I rose to my feet, I remembered the confused bickering and babbling of the men, I rose time and time again, but it seemed, they too mirrored my resilience, it was unnatural but finally, one by one they fell."

He grew silent and began to mop the tears that tumbled down the crevices on his face; "By the time I was done fighting I was nearly dead, dripping with blood and sweat, but I was stubborn, I needed to find her, I never managed to until the next morning. I found her cold dead body; a spear planted in her chest, I was the only survivor, amid all the skirmish," the man said as he began to shake the tears that flowed profusely from his face.

"I knelt in that spot for hours, dazed and confused, eventually I managed to gather the strength and crawled back to the pool, I dived into the water in desperation, sank to the bottom broken and bruised, and I rose to the surface healed, it was then I realized the true power of the water; to heal and sustain life. The days that followed, I tried long and hard to justify my actions but my anger subsided, and reason took root and blossomed a conscience and guilt. The screams of Ayma and her people, they haunted my thoughts, their faces were in my dreams. I had this foolish notion of doing good, maybe that would quell the guilt, be penance, so I could be forgiven. But it never stopped, and my good deeds became more extravagant and grandstanding."

76

The man stopped to clean his nose and mop his face, "I settled here not too far from the pool, the water extended my life, didn't keep me young though, but no amount of good I did ever absolve my guilt and self-hate."

After these words, a long silence ensued, Eli simply rose his hand and reached for the man's shoulder. Carefully Eli sifted through his mind to find words to ease the man's pain. "I... remember, when the news of my court matter reached home, I don't think I was ever so scared. I ran away from home so many times, broke mum's heart each time, I was scared of what was in store for me, even now I thought of running away from here," he said trying to hide his flushed cheeks. "I think the hardest thing for me to do was accept that my actions got me here." The man halted his whimpering and grew silent focusing his teary red eyes on Eli as he spoke.

"Every time mum and pops found me, no matter how far I went or how well I hid, mum would say each time, look you did what you did, the consequence you must now face, there is no running from that, accept it and face it," Elias said.

The man's face grew blank in amazement, "I taught her that," he said slowly. He covered his face for a moment, then said, moving his hands from over his lips, "What a hypocrite, I am telling you about consequence, telling you about your actions, when I have been running from damnation, I have been running for so long boy, now I have no choice but to face it." Eli sensed a sad reassurance in his voice.

"About the lake?" Eli said with some concern, "This was the last of it, the pool dried months ago," said the man sadly.

Eli dipped his head and exhaled in disappointment.

The old man rose to his feet, looking down at Eli, he said, "When you think of doing something stupid, remember what I told you in great detail, every word, every action, think of the old fool who thought he could run from it, think of the fool who thought water could wash it away, and should you forget it, remember your mother's words; you could never run from it, the consequence," the old man said, grabbing unto the boy's shoulder tautly.

Eli rose to his feet and looked to the man's face, his eyes were swollen from crying and at his words he bowed his head.

"Give me your word that you'll tell no one of this, and remember my words, and do better than me." Eli's great-great-grandfather instilled once more.

"You have my word," Eli said.

"Hurry now, let's go inside," the old man murmured as he picked up the lantern and handed it to Eli, and said, "Lead the way." Slowly, the two walked back to the veranda, the old man halted at the stairs and clenched the wooden railing and said, "You go inside, I just need some air for a bit, remind me to call your mother tomorrow, okay, and Eli, thank you."

"Eli bobbed his head and walked to the door, he carefully placed the lantern on the wooden floor of the veranda, but before he went inside, he took one final look at Pa, who turned slowly to look at the sky. He took a deep breath and fought hard to keep the tears from flowing from his eyes, he quickly withdrew and went to his room.

The old man stood and lifted his eyes to the sky, his sight grew blurry and he could feel the strength begin to leave him.

GLOSSARY

Aye - Hello, or a means of getting someone's attention

Deus animam meam - Latin meaning, My God

Eh - Dialect for not, did not, didn't or no. Could also be used to emphasize a point

Hun - shorten dialect version of Honey

Imps - used as an insult, meaning inferior or weak

Oye - Hello, or a means of getting someone's attention

Yuh- a dialect form of you

Si - Yes in Spanish

Oui – Yes in French

Merci – Thank you in French

Treinta – Thirty in Spanish

CPSIA information can be obtained
at www.ICGtesting.com
Printed in the USA
BVHW041256030521
606340BV00009B/2672